THE LONG RIDE

DEL PRATT

The Long Ride
Copyright © 2023 by Del Pratt

All rights reserved. No part of this publication
may be reproduced, distributed, or transmitted
in any form or by any means, including
photocopying, recording, or other electronic
or mechanical methods, without the prior
written permission of the author, except
in the case of brief quotations embodied
in critical reviews and certain other non-
commercial uses permitted by copyright law.

Tellwell Talent
www.tellwell.ca

ISBN
978-1-998190-32-4 (Hardcover)
978-1-998190-31-7 (Paperback)
978-1-998190-33-1 (eBook)
978-1-998190-34-8 (Audiobook)

DEDICATION

I would like to dedicate this book to two people. Firstly, my mother, Phyllis Pratt. When a little boy in Grade 2 came home from school and wanted a book to read, Mom gave me a Western she had on hand. I started reading books then and have never stopped.

I would also like to dedicate this to my high school English teacher, Georgia Sullivan, who planted a tiny seed over forty years ago. When I started writing cowboy poetry fifteen years ago, that seed started to grow. And with this book, that plant is starting to bloom.

Thanks to you both,

Del

Acknowledgements

I would like to acknowledge and thank my wife, Sheila Rae Andersen. Who would have known when we met on the first day of Grade 10 back in 1977 that we would end up getting married thirty-six years later!

She has fully supported and encouraged me from the start to the finish of this project, including having it published. This book would not have been possible without her countless hours of work and her ideas. Many thanks to her for putting up with this grumpy old cowboy, who had to swallow his pride a few times during the various stages of editing. I know that, between the two of us, we made a better book.

I would also like to thank Dr. Peter Scott for his invaluable expertise, proofreading, and insights. And express my appreciation to Cathy Buchanan, Georgia Sullivan, Tim Westerlund, and Dale Pratt for your support for all of my work and especially your encouragement after reading this manuscript.

AUTHOR'S NOTE

The Long Ride is a Western historical adventure novel that takes place in Western Canada in 1865, which at that time was still known as Rupert's Land. This was a very interesting era in Western Canadian history. At this time, the Indigenous tribes are still living on their traditional lands, hunting and trading. The Metis have their way of life—hunting buffalo, trading, and farming in the French tradition. Governor William McTavish is the governor of both the Red River Colony (the area around what is now known as Winnipeg) and Rupert's Land. Within ten short years, all of this will have changed drastically.

While the main characters in *The Long Ride* are fictional, all other details in the story are historically accurate: Governor William McTavish, the Indigenous tribes, the places, the trails, the forts, even the dilapidated scow of a ferry at Fort Garry! I'm hoping this book gives the reader a chance to learn more about this fascinating time in Western Canadian history while enjoying a rollicking adventure story with plenty of action!

Map designed by Chengis Javeri

CHAPTER ONE

It was Old Moses who saved our hides. He'd been a couple horse lengths ahead and to the right of me; Pa had been a little left and behind. As I recall, Moses had yelled "DOWN," and all three of us kicked out of our stirrups and dove for the ground. As we were finding out how deep we could dive on land, the shrill whistling and loud whining of bullets sounded overhead, quickly followed by a volley of loud gunshots.

We'd been ambushed. But through the combination of luck, intuition, and the savvy of an old mountain man, we were still in the game. We had been in the process of crossing a dry water run when the shooting started. All three of us had managed to scramble to the lowest spot we could find for cover while our would-be killers were reloading. We had about twenty seconds before there was a whine over our heads, followed by another loud boom.

"A .58-calibre rifle musket; probably an Enfield that time. They'll keep our heads down with a couple of muskets while some of them try to flank us from both sides." That was Pa talking, and seeing as he had just served in Mr. Lincoln's army for four years, I figured he knew what he was talking about.

Our horses and pack mule trotted back about three hundred yards and started grazing. They'd be fine, for now. Our bushwhackers would be counting on coming out of this with them and our kit.

Moses scratched his white stubble of a beard while looking over at Pa. "I'm a figurin' there's about six, maybe seven, by the sound of them bullets, but what in tarnation was that shrill whistling? I was shot at a lot of times out in the mountains but never heard anything like that before!"

"Reb sniper rifle. I've seen men killed at a thousand yards with them," answered Pa. "What say we make the odds a little better and maybe get out of this mess."

Moses pondered a minute or two and then started talking. "Here's the way I see it. Those boys want to get this done with quick. They're a little impatient. Made too many mistakes. They didn't stay back far enough in that grove of trees. One of their guns gave a little glint of reflection. The fact we were riding toward them in the late morning was luck on our part." Another zing went over us, followed by a loud boom. Looking at me with his piercing blue eyes as he pulled the ramrod from his rifle, Moses said, "Take my hat and put it on this. I'll belly down in the grass along this water run to the left for about thirty yards. Your Pa'll go right about the same distance. Once we're outta sight, count to three hundred, then raise the ramrod and let out a big war whoop."

Then looking to Pa, he said, "You ready, William?"

Pa nodded, and they started crawling slow, going their separate ways in the little water run. I could see them for a few minutes, but they soon faded into the lush grass. Now, it was time to start counting. I tried to count reasonably slow, though with my heart pounding about 150 beats a minute, it wasn't easy! In all my seventeen years, this was the first time I had ever been shot at. It had only been five minutes at the most since we'd bailed off our horses, but the world seemed to slow right down for me. I kept counting, and finally… 298… 299… 300! I raised Moses's battered old felt hat on that ramrod and let out an almighty holler. And all hell broke loose!

There was a ziiing of a bullet going over my head, a shrill whistling, another zing, followed by the loud rolling boom of multiple guns. Then a kaboom that I knew was Moses's old mountain rifle, quickly followed by the sharp crack of Pa's Warner carbine and more sharp bangs of pistols firing. The sulphur smell of burnt gunpowder hung heavily in the air.

I hauled down the ramrod and hat—no bullet hole in the hat—and in about fifteen minutes, Pa was back beside me. After another couple of minutes, we saw Moses' white shock of hair moving toward us through the grass, and then he was back with us. "There was two of 'em. One's dead, the other was hit hard."

Pa was still breathing heavily, trying to regain his breath. "There was a couple on my side, too. One got excited and shot at your hat, giving away their position. I put a bullet in one with the carbine and a couple of pistol balls in the other. I was close enough to see they are both goners."

Pa looked at me. "You okay, Jimmy?"

Still in shock, I nodded. And then said shakily as the realization set in, "We could've been killed!"

Moses grinned at me. "We weren't though, Jimmy, and that's what matters. Now we gotta wait a while. Those boys in the trees will start to figure out the odds ain't as good." Then he took his ramrod and commenced loading his old rifle while lying on his back. He set the hammer at half cock, poured powder in the end of the barrel, then tipped it up a bit, tapped the butt, took a greased patch out of the patch box, wrapped it around a lead ball, and pushed it into the end of the barrel. He then used the ramrod to drive the ball and seat it against the powder charge. Next, he reached into his possible bag, which held all the accessories needed for his rifle and pistol, pulled out a cap, and put it on the nipple under the hammer. He repeated the process with his .54-calibre pistol.

Pa started reloading his Colt pistol. He poured a measure out of his powder flask into a chamber in the revolving cylinder, put a greased ball in the chamber, and seated the ball down on to the powder with the lever under the barrel of the pistol. Repeating this process for each chamber he had fired, he then put a cap on each. The Colt had six chambers. You loaded five and carried it with the hammer on the empty one so a hard bump wouldn't fire the gun. Pa had already reloaded the Warner carbine. It was one of them new breech-loading cartridge guns issued to the cavalry during the war.

Seeing as I hadn't fired a shot, my Warner was still loaded. Pa saw me looking at him. "We'll hunker down in this grass for an hour or so. Those boys will either get impatient and make another slip up, or they'll cut their losses and run. Just try to rest. We'll let you know if anything happens. It's not the worst pickle Ol' Moses and

I have been in." Then he added, "These boys ain't near as good as the Blackfoot or the Ree, and they never got our scalps. We'll come out of this just fine."

I knew he was trying to keep me from getting too nervous, but this was my first shooting scrape. My heart was slowing down, and the excitement was wearing off. To keep my mind occupied, I started thinking back to how we had ended up in a shallow water run with lead flying over our heads in the first place.

Chapter Two

I guess it started a little over four years ago when the southern states seceded from the union. President Lincoln had called for 75,000 volunteers for ninety days to put down the rebellion. After the wheat and oats were planted, Pa volunteered, figuring he would be home by fall. He got home four years later.

When Pa had gone off to war, he had left Ol' Moses in charge of the farm and Grandma in charge of the house, with my fifteen-year-old sister Judith and thirteen-year-old me as helpers.

We lived in western Minnesota, where the prairie met the forest, and there were open spaces of grassland. We had homesteaded on good productive land with a creek running through it and had plenty of trees nearby for wood. All figured, we were building us a pretty good farm. We had to work hard, but we never went hungry.

We could even trade a little, as we were only a couple of miles off what was known as the Woods Trail. This was a route that Red River carts used to haul freight from Saint Paul to Fort Garry and the Red River settlements up in Rupert's Land. These carts were made using only wood and hide, no metal. The axles were not greased, as dust would stick to the wood and wear it down like sandpaper. Even so, the axles would wear. We always knew when a group of carts was on the trail. You could hear them more than a mile away most days, as their ungreased axles sounded like a fiddle out of tune.

That's where our trading came in. It was Moses who came up with the idea. He cut down some oak trees and split them into manageable pieces. After a year of seasoning, he cut and split rough axles that we could then use to trade for dry goods, tools, etc. Being able to trade with the freighters as they passed through meant that we didn't have to make the long trip to St. Paul.

Moses was a survivor. Of average height and slight of build, he was pure muscle and rawhide. He had been a mountain man back in the days of the fur trade, and his leathery face was permanently tanned from years of exposure to sun and wind. Moses wasn't his given name. The other trappers had started calling him Moses when his hair had gone snow white in his early twenties, making him look much older. He still wore it long, like when he was in the mountains. He'd gone west from Saint Louis to trap beaver with Ashley's first brigade in the early 1820s. He'd trapped, traded, and fought Indians with the likes of Joe Meek and the Sublette brothers. Brokenhand Fitzpatrick had been one of his friends.

Wanting a change, he had brought his furs to Saint Louis in the late spring of 1831. And that's where he met Grandma and her ten-year-old son William, who grew up to be my Pa. Moses and Grandma never really talked much about how they met or what had happened to Pa's father. All I knew was that they were married that fall.

Pa had met our mother in the early '40s when he and Moses were hired as scouts for a wagon train going to the Oregon Country. Pa had been scouting a few days ahead of the wagons and had been waiting at the evening campsite when the first wagons rolled up. One of the wagons had been driven by a pretty young lady with long blonde hair and sparkling blue eyes. Moses told me it was love at first sight for both.

For the first few years of their marriage, they lived in a small town outside St. Louis. Pa and Moses continued to make a living scouting for wagon trains while Grandma stayed with our mother. In the early 1850s, our family—which had now grown to include my older sister Judith and me—filed on a homestead in the wilderness of Minnesota. Pa and Moses built a sturdy log cabin for our family of six to live in.

It was here that our mother took sick and passed away when I was six. Pa took it pretty hard. Grandma was the glue that held our family together. She was barely five feet tall but was a force to be reckoned with. She was always in motion, from the time she got up to when she went to bed. Even though she had had plenty of hard times, she had never given up.

Judith was only two years older than me. After our mother died, she became a mother hen to me, and we were pretty much inseparable. Like a lot of frontier kids, me and Judith had to grow up quick, especially when Pa went away to war for four years.

By the time Pa rode off to the war, I was old enough to help with the farming. Moses had already taught both Judith and me to shoot and hunt. He took us out into the forest one at a time, and we would practice loading and firing his old mountain rifle. It was a .54-calibre full-stocked long rifle made in Nazareth, Pennsylvania. It was originally a flintlock, but Moses had converted it to use percussion caps in the early '30s.

When he wasn't teaching us hunting skills, he taught us survival skills—how to make a shelter, build a fire, tan a deer hide, and a hundred other things.

Grandma, on the other hand, insisted we learn how to read and write. *Properly*. She had a couple of old books and, of course, a Bible. We had no church anywhere near us, but between Judith and me, we about near wore out that Bible learning to read. Grandma figured that even I had to learn how to cook a little bit. Judith was a natural—her biscuits were pure "heaven in a pan," whereas mine would have made good cannon balls if we'd had a cannon.

A year after Pa went east to the rebellion, there was a Sioux uprising in Minnesota. While he was fighting in the war between the States, at home we had an Indian war to deal with. Moses had spent a lot of time living amongst Indians in the west and by and large, got along with them, except the Arikara (usually called Rees by the mountain men) and the Blackfoot. I had always figured we were left alone by the Sioux because Moses treated them with respect and was honest when we traded with them. After all, the whole uprising was caused by the tribe not getting the rations they had been promised by the treaty Little Crow had made with the US Government. As events were to unfold, and I was to learn more about the old man, I realized that maybe those Sioux knew more about Moses than I did.

May 10, 1865, was the happiest day of my life. I looked down the trail from our yard and saw a cavalry man riding toward us. His brown hair was now sprinkled with grey, his broad shoulders were stooped a little, and he was thinner than I remembered. But I knew immediately that it was Pa. And he was home!

I started hollering, "Pa's home!" and everybody came running out. We had the happiest reunion you could imagine.

Now that the war was over and Pa was home for good, he could tell us what he'd actually been doing during the war. He had sent letters occasionally and had even been home for a short furlough in '63, but he had never said much.

When the war had broken out, Pa had gone east and joined a cavalry outfit. The unit had an old major training them, and when he had learned Pa had been a scout, a trapper, and could read and write, things started to happen. To make a long story short, that old major became a colonel, then a brigadier general, and finally a major general in command of a corps. He had made Pa an officer on his staff early on. Pa was with him the entire war, serving as his intelligence officer—going behind the Rebel lines with a small troop of horse soldiers and gathering intelligence.

Pa had been sitting in the shade of a big old elm tree having a smoke the day after Lee surrendered at Appomattox Court House. The old general walked up to Pa with some papers in his hand. "Come with me, Captain," the old general had said. They started walking toward some supply wagons that had just rolled in.

"Captain, do you have any idea how much money was made by profiteers during this war?" Pa had reckoned a lot, but he didn't know how much. Looking at Pa, the general had said, "Millions of dollars. And now that it's over, some of those same people will make money selling off the army's surplus."

They stopped at a wagon loaded with crates of new carbines for the cavalry. "It will take a few days to shut the supply chain down, Captain. Some think we will have to take this army to North Carolina to help Billy Sherman finish off General Johnson, but I'm pretty sure Johnson will surrender in a few days before we are needed. The South has lost, and he knows it."

Handing Pa the papers, he took a pry bar and forced the lid off a crate. He reached in and pulled out a new breech-loading Warner carbine. Looking at Pa he said, "I haven't forgotten all the times your intelligence-gathering made a difference. Or the time you saved my headquarters from Wade Hampton's cavalry. These carbines will not even be issued. Living on the frontier, you can use two of these carbines, so take them and all the cartridges you want. Take a good horse, your McClellan saddle, a pack mule, two weeks' rations, and your Colt pistol. Those papers you're holding are your discharge papers and bills of sale. I went to Grant and had him sign everything. You won't be having any trouble with the provost guard."

He shook Pa's hand as he said, "Thank you, William. You've seen enough elephants. Now get home to your family."

And that's how Pa managed to come home with two brand new breech-loading Warner carbines in 56-50 calibre, a .45 Colt pistol, a good bay gelding, a saddle, and a sturdy if somewhat ornery mule with a pack saddle.

Pa had come through Saint Paul on his way home. He had loaded Rosie's pack saddle (he'd named the mule Rosie on account of her "sweet" disposition) with some of the basic supplies that he had figured we would need: flour, sugar, yeast, baking powder, coffee, tobacco, and some canned peaches. He had also picked up a few yards of cloth and notions for Grandma and Judith to make new dresses.

Grandma and Judith were looking at all the material and supplies. "How did you afford all this?"

Pa smiled at them, saying, "For the last twenty-six months of the war, I was a captain. That meant I got paid a hundred and fifteen dollars a month. There is still two thousand dollars in a bank in Saint Paul, over and above what I left with you in '63."

Moses chimed in, "And we still got a little of that left."

As far as Pa was concerned, every dime of that money was to be used for the good of the family. He explained, "I was thinking on maybe making the house a little bigger. We could cut logs for the walls and buy lumber for the roof and the floor. Possibly buy some cattle, a couple more horses, and maybe even a mower."

We talked late into the night, catching up. But when morning came, Pa was ready to get planting, working on corrals, and generally doing what needed doing on the farm. With three men working (at seventeen, I considered myself a man now), the spring work was getting caught up. We got a few acres of corn seeded and some wheat for a cash crop. We put in some oats for the stock and planted an acre of garden. It was more garden than we needed to feed ourselves, but we figured with all the Red River carts on the trail going north later in the summer, they would be quite happy to trade for some fresh vegetables.

Chapter Three

We had finally finished all of our planting and were sitting in the shade of our front porch late afternoon one day when a young man rode up the trail to our yard. He was a big man with a thick mop of blond hair, bright blue eyes, and a friendly smile, who looked to be about twenty-five years old. Looking down at us from his horse and speaking with a Danish accent, he greeted us, saying, "I'm Ollie Johansen. I've taken out a homestead four miles west. I just finished breaking some land yesterday and thought maybe I should go around and meet my neighbours."

Pa looked up at Ollie and said, "Climb on down and come sit in the shade. I'm William Munro, this is my son Jimmy, and that old 'he-coon' with the Green River in his hand is James Munro, but everyone calls him Moses."

I looked over at Moses, and sure enough, that old knife was in his hand. He didn't survive in the Rocky Mountains with a full head of hair by being trusting of his fellow man. If Ollie had reached for a gun, that old knife would've been half buried in his chest before he even knew what happened.

As it turned out, Ollie was as good a fellow as you would ever want to meet.

Pa started the conversation, asking, "What regiment were you in, Ollie?" The faded blue pants had been a dead giveaway to Pa.

Ollie looked up at Pa and replied, "First Minnesota, sir. I was wounded at Petersburg a month before the war ended. I remember you now, Captain. It was at night. I was on picket duty when a shot-up cavalry patrol returned through our lines. We'd been told you might be returning. As I recall, you had a prisoner."

Pa was quiet for a few seconds. "Yes, that was me and some of my men. That prisoner was one of Lee's couriers. He had letters from Lee to Jefferson Davis on him."

Ollie looked at Pa. "Guess we've both seen all the elephants we will ever want to see." (Pa later explained to me that "seeing the elephant" was what the soldiers called having been in combat. He also told me the First Minnesota, the regiment that Ollie had served with, suffered 82 percent casualties on the second day at Gettysburg. When their three-year term was up in '64, most had rejoined to see the war through).

We had been jawing with him for a while when suddenly Ollie stopped talking, and his eyes opened wide. I turned and saw that Judith had stepped out onto the porch. At that moment, I could see her through Ollie's eyes, and I realized that my sister had grown into a beautiful young woman. She was wearing the new dress she and Grandma had made. With shining blonde hair that flowed over her shoulders and blue eyes that sparkled when she smiled, even I had to admit she was as pretty as a picture.

Pa looked over at Judith, trying to hide his surprise, and said, "Ollie Johansen, meet my daughter, Judith."

Ollie was a little awestruck, especially when Judith smiled at him, saying, "A pleasure, Mr. Johansen. Would you like to stay for dinner? We have lots, and I baked a peach pie this morning."

I don't know how they did it, but in the time since Ollie rode up, Grandma and Judith almost had dinner ready, and Judith had found time to change into that new dress.

Well, Ollie was no fool, for sure. Before long, we were all sitting down at the table, enjoying a feast as good as anything served to Queen Victoria herself. Grandma made sure Ollie knew how much of the dinner Judith had made. You'd have thought all she did was watch Judith cook. I knew better. Knew enough to keep quiet, too.

The conversation turned to our farms and future plans and how we seemed to be getting a few more neighbours moving in. I noticed Judith and Ollie hardly took their eyes off each other the whole time.

When it came time to head home, Ollie stood up, saying, "Thank you, ladies. That was a mighty fine meal." Smiling at Judith, he added, "That is the best peach pie I've ever had."

Judith smiled back, answering, "You are most welcome, Mr. Johansen."

Now, I'm no expert on such matters, but looking back, I think Ollie's fate was sealed by the time he left. If Judith's downright pleasant appearance hadn't caught his attention enough, that dinner and peach pie sure did. She may not have had a saddle on him yet, but she sure had him halter broke.

As the spring turned to summer, Ollie seemed to be showing up quite often—once or even twice a week. I noticed that Grandma always made sure to invite Ollie in for a bite to eat, and Judith was all smiles when he was there.

As I recall, Ollie was even at our place when Pa got the letter. There had been a post office set up at a homesteader's house to the southeast of us, and Moses had made the two-day ride to get the mail.

Moses rode up the trail to our yard. He met Pa in front of the house and handed him a letter. Pa looked at the envelope, frowned, and then tucked it away in his pocket. At the time, I didn't think much of it.

There was a letter for Grandma from her sister, who lived in Chicago, and a few issues of Harper's Weekly. Pa had gotten used to reading it during the war and had arranged to have it sent out to us. When I asked Pa about his letter, he looked up and said it was from someone he'd been in the army with. Old Moses just kind of nodded to me, and so I let it be.

In late July, Ollie rode up and asked to speak to Pa in private. We had shut down for the day after putting up some hay. Moses looked at me, saying, "Jimmy, let's go check on the fence out back of the house." He had a bit of a grin. We were both pretty sure what Ollie wanted to talk to Pa about. I had kind of wanted to stick around and see this.

Pa and Ollie were still on the front step when Moses and I got back from checking a perfectly good fence.

Judith stepped out to the porch, looked at Pa, and he nodded. She gave a little yelp of joy, and she and Ollie beamed at each other. She happily went to stand beside him, linking her arm through his. Grandma came out of the house, took in the scene, went over to Judith and Ollie, and gave them each a big hug. Moses and I shook hands with Ollie, and we all went inside.

We visited and made plans till the late hours. Pa even brought out a bottle of whisky from Scotland that he had gotten home without breaking. He said it was for a special occasion, and this definitely qualified. The sun was coming up when Ollie finally headed off for home.

The wedding party was on the last day of July at our place, and it was quite the event. Back then, folks would gather from miles around to attend a good shindig. People had been moving into the area, a few at a time, since the war ended. Why, there must have been over fifty people there, including the preacher that Moses had fetched from a settlement a couple days ride to the southeast.

Judith was wearing our mother's wedding gown, which Grandma had stored away all these years. She had tiny purple flowers woven through her hair and was beaming with happiness. Folks said she was one of the prettiest brides they had ever seen. Ollie was in his best pair of pants, freshly ironed, and his white shirt, with his blond hair neatly parted and combed.

The preacher started the wedding by reading scripture from Grandma's family Bible. He then had Judith and Ollie join hands, and they recited their vows. When he pronounced them man and wife, the crowd started cheering.

And then—it was time for the feast! Everybody brought some grub of some kind. And let me tell you, those ladies could cook. There was roast venison, fried chicken, cooked wild rice, all kinds of fresh vegetables that were ready in the gardens—potatoes, carrots, cucumbers, tomatoes, peas, onions. And the baking! Freshly made buns and bread, blueberry and apple pies. And to top things off, Grandma had baked a wedding cake and decorated it with wild strawberries.

After we ate, Ollie brought out some Danish aquavit and offered the men a drink. Then the music began. One old boy had a fiddle, and another, who was a vet, had brought a cigar box banjo that he had made during the war. Their lively renditions of songs such as "Turkey in the Straw" and "Oh! Susannah" soon had all the folks up dancing.

The festivities carried on until the sun was up. Folks were getting ready to head home until Grandma started cooking some pancakes. No one had ever left my grandma's place hungry, and that included now.

By noon, everyone had headed back to their homesteads. It had been a great celebration and a good chance to get to know more of our neighbours. Little did I know how soon we would be counting on them.

Chapter Four

A few days after the wedding party, we had set about cutting a few acres of some native grass that was a half mile from the house. This was hard work with a scythe, but it was doing work like this that helped put some strength in my shoulders. It took us three long days to get that grass cut, but it looked like we would have enough to feed our horses through the winter. It had to dry for a few more days before we could stack it, so Pa figured it might be a good time for me to ride over to Ollie and Judith's place to see if they needed a hand with anything.

I saddled the roan mare and grabbed the Warner carbine that Pa had given me, thinking I might get a chance at a young buck. We could always dry the meat, and a good deer hide had a lot of uses.

I was in no hurry, so I didn't get to their place until a little after noon. Riding into the yard, I started to get a bad feeling. As I approached the house, I could see the door hanging raggedly from one hinge, with the frame splintered—as if somebody had kicked it in. Mud had been tracked all over the porch and in through the front door. The whole place was dead quiet.

I climbed down off my horse and unslung my carbine. I pulled the hammer back and carefully stepped onto the porch, constantly looking all around. I peered into the dim light of the open doorway and was immediately hit by a decaying stench—the smell of death. My body wanted to run, but I knew I had to see who it was. I stepped inside the doorway, and a cloud of flies buzzed over me. I made my way over to take a closer look at the bloated body and heaved a sigh of relief. It wasn't Judith or Ollie.

It was a man in a faded and worn blue uniform. He had taken a large bullet right through the chest, which had knocked him down onto his back. The entire front of his shirt was stained with dried blood. Crows or maybe magpies had already swooped in and picked out his eyes. Maggots were squirming from the wound. Death had come quick to him.

It wasn't the first dead body I had seen. But I had never seen one that looked like this before. Fighting down the urge to heave my guts out, I picked my way around the body to check out the rest of the house. I knew I had to keep looking for Judith and Ollie.

Growing up with Judith, I knew she always had things tidy and neat—everything in its place. But now the whole place was a disaster. The dinner table had been flung onto its side, broken dishes scattered around it. The shelves were empty; all of the dry goods had been stolen. And mud was tracked through everywhere.

Finding no sign of anyone in the house, I went back outside. And threw up as soon as I got out the door. Gulping in some fresh air, I then cautiously made my way over to the barn. The large door gaped open. All three of Ollie's horses were gone, and the pegs holding their bridles and harness were empty. There was no sign of Ollie's wagon.

Ollie had been fattening up two hogs. They had both been shot in their pen and dragged out into the middle of the barn. It looked like they had been roughly butchered with the good cuts of meat taken, but the scavengers—coyotes, crows, and magpies—had obviously been feeding for a few days, and there wasn't much left.

Still no sign of Judith and Ollie. Where on earth were they? What had happened to them? I was feeling sick again, but now with dread. Whatever had happened, I knew I needed Moses and Pa.

I threw myself on the back of the roan and hightailed it for home. That mare loved to run, and I let her. She was as surefooted a horse as a man could ever want. I had to duck a few times under tree branches and hang on when she jumped the creek, but she sure did her part getting us home in a hurry.

I galloped into the yard on my lathered-up horse and started hollering for Pa as loud as I could. Grandma flew out on the porch, and Pa and Moses came running up to the house from the barn.

"What's wrong?" Pa urgently demanded.

I gasped, "Judith and Ollie are gone! Someone hit their place. There's a dead guy on the floor in the house. Their horses and wagon are gone. The hogs were killed. It's really bad, Pa."

Pa's face flashed with anger. Then he squared his jaw and grimly declared, "We've got to go after them." I hadn't noticed, but while I was telling Pa all this, Moses and Grandma had gone inside the house. Now they came back out.

Moses had his mountain rifle, Green River, tomahawk, and his pistol. His powder horn and possible bag hung over his shoulder from their straps. He looked at Pa, saying, "I'll saddle the horses; you grab your gear."

We raced out of our yard in less than five minutes, and in no time were galloping into Ollie's homestead. We stopped and dismounted about fifty yards from the house. Me, being the least experienced, held the horses while Pa and Moses looked for sign of who or what had gone down here.

Pa went into the house while Moses checked over the barn and outlying areas. Pa came out and walked over to me. "We'll wait till Moses is done with the yard, and then we'll figure out what we need to do."

Ten minutes later, Moses joined us. "This is a bad bunch, boys. Going by all the footprints, I'm thinking there's fifteen to twenty of them. They left their horses back in the trees and snuck into the yard on foot. I'm pretty sure they have Judith with them. I think she shot the jasper in the house. It looks like they got to Ollie in the barn. Wagon and team are gone. There are two different places in the barn with blood. Looks to me like Ollie got a pitchfork into one, but he got shot in the process. There's no sign of Ollie or anyone else anywhere, so I think he's maybe followin' them, even with a bullet in him. Going by the uniform on the dead guy in the house, this bunch are likely Union deserters."

Looking at Pa, he said, "William, judging by the maggots and how the grass has come back up over their tracks, I think they've already got four days on us. If we're gonna catch up to Judith, we don't have time to go to Saint Paul for the marshal. We gotta go after them ourselves."

Pa nodded. "It'll be dark in an hour. How 'bout I start tracking them? You two go back home and get the mule and load her up with supplies and our bed rolls. More lead, powder, caps, and cartridges for the carbines, too. Pack salve and lots of clean rags for bandages."

Pa then looked at me. "Jimmy, ride to the Olsens. Tell them what's happened and that we'll be going after Judith. Ask if they could look after things while we're gone. They have a big family. I'm hoping maybe one of their older girls could stay with your grandma."

Moses nodded to Pa. "We'll leave early. Hope to catch up with you in a couple of days."

With that, we split up. Pa headed north, following the wagon tracks. Moses and I started riding back to the farm to get everything we would be needing. For the first time since I had seen Judith's door hanging from the broken hinge, I had time to think about what had happened. Who on earth would do something like this? Why had they taken Judith? Where were they going with her? Where was Ollie? I was sick with worry. I could see Moses was feeling mighty bad, too.

We'd ridden about a mile when Moses started talking. "Gonna be a long trail gettin' Judith back. Huntin' men ain't like huntin' deer. Deer don't try to kill you. You'll be learning more things faster in the next few days than you've ever learned before. Always pay attention to everything around you. Once we hit that trail, there will never be a time that we can let our guard down."

He looked at me and continued in a serious voice. "I was about your age when I headed to the mountains with Ashley's first fur brigade. I learned fast. There will come a time on this ride when we'll have to kill. Judging by the dead guy in the house, this group is probably a bunch of leftover deserters from the war. They've lost any decency they might have had. Men like these won't give up without a fight.

"You'd best cut over to the Olsen's place now. I'll see you at home."

We split up, and in less than an hour, I was at the Olsens.

I commenced to telling Mr. Olsen the whole story (his given name was Marten, but in those days, you called your elders Mr. and Mrs.). He wanted to grab his rifle and go with us right then and there, but when I told him how Pa wanted him to look after our place and Grandma, he realized it was best if he stayed.

He promised to look after things, and I knew he meant it. On the frontier, folks tended to look out for each other. It was called surviving.

It was past dark when I got home. After giving my horse a rub down, I went into the house. Grandma had been busy while we were gone. Pretty much everything we needed was already neatly piled up on the kitchen floor.

Moses looked at me. "Better hit the hay, Jimmy. We'll be moving early."

The sun was starting to glow in the east as we rode out of the yard. We had gotten up before daybreak and fed the horses some oats. Moses wanted them well-fed and well-rested before we hit the trail.

Grandma was teary-eyed when we said our goodbyes. She was the rock that got our family through everything that had happened since Ma had passed, but this was pushing even her limits.

She looked up at us on our horses. "Bring our girl home, Moses. And Jimmy, you be sure and listen to your Pa and Moses." With that, she turned and went back into the house.

We hit the trail—an old mountain man, a boy on the edge of manhood, two good saddle horses, and one ornery pack mule.

CHAPTER FIVE

We caught up to Pa in the midafternoon. When we rode up, we could see that he was kneeling beside Ollie! Pa turned to us and spoke. "I'm sure glad to see you two. I found Ollie here, collapsed in the grass, a few hours ago. He's still alive, but he's in rough shape. He's got a pistol ball in him, just above the left hip. I covered him with my bedroll and made him as comfortable as I could. He's had a rough go of it. By the look of his hands and knees, he started to crawl when he couldn't walk any more. Even though he managed to plug the bullet hole himself with some moss, he's lost a lot of blood. He just kept on following the wagon tracks until he passed out."

Looking at Moses, he asked, "Did you fellas pack a bottle of that rubbing alcohol?"

I slid off my horse and got the bottle out of the pack that was on Rosie. Pa had bought this bottle in Saint Paul on his way home. He had learned a lot about treating gunshot wounds in the past four years. I got him a small clean rag, and he soaked it in alcohol and commenced to clean the wound as best he could. By now, Ollie was out cold, so Pa wanted to work quickly before he woke up.

Moses reached over my shoulder from behind and put two wire knitting needles in my hand. "Soak these in that alcohol, Jimmy."

I looked up at him, wondering where these had come from.

He looked back at me and winked. "Not the first time your grandma's had her menfolk head out on a war trail."

When Pa finished cleaning the wound and surrounding area, he reached up and took one of the knitting needles and probed for the bullet. When he found it, he reached for the second needle, and with the two needles, he managed to work out the bullet.

Pouring a little more of the alcohol on the wound, he looked up at me. I handed him the needle and thread Moses had put in my hand while Pa was digging out the bullet. After he had sewn up the wound, he put on some of the beeswax-based salve that Grandma had sent.

Fortunately, we were still in an area where groves of aspen were scattered amongst the tall prairie grass. We only had to move Ollie about fifty yards to where we could make a shelter. Moses used his tomahawk to cut down some saplings for poles, and with the canvas tarp we had brought with us, he soon had a lean-to built. Even though it was hot during the day, being early August, it got cooler at night, so Pa kept Ollie wrapped with one of our bedrolls.

I picketed the horses and gathered up a whack of firewood from all the dead fall. Once we had a good fire going, I commenced making supper while Pa helped finish the shelter.

When we'd eaten, Pa said to me, "Jimmy, you take first watch. Moses will take second watch around two, and I'll take the last watch. Just in case any of those renegades decide to check out their back trail."

As I moved around quietly the campsite, I couldn't help but worry. Where was Judith? What was happening to her? If she could just hang on until we get to her. Ollie was in no shape to ride anywhere. How could we catch up to the kidnappers when we needed to look after him?

I checked on Ollie every time I made a circuit. Toward the end of my watch, I noticed that, even though he hadn't awoken since Pa removed the bullet, his breathing seemed to be getting a little steadier and stronger.

Moses was up and waiting for me before I even figured it was his turn. I realized he had probably not really gotten to sleep on my first night of being on watch. "Get some shut-eye, Jimmy. Gonna be a long day tomorrow."

I laid down, and I hate to admit it—what with Judith being kidnapped and Ollie being shot and all—but I crashed and slept like a log.

When I awoke, the sun was just starting to rise in the east. Pa and Moses were figuring out what to do with Ollie. I could hear Pa saying, "His breathing is a little better, but laying down, his lungs will start to get fluid in them. Seen it many times in the war."

I looked over at Moses, and I could see him in deep thought. "What if we make a travois and have the mule haul it? The slope will help Ollie's breathing, and it would make him movable. As much as it's going to hurt him, we can't wait here. We gotta keep going after Judith." After pausing for a few seconds, he said, "We are close enough to the Woods Trail we might meet up with a brigade of Metis traders going to Saint Paul. Maybe get lucky and even meet up with one of the fellers I know. Couple of them might be able to take Ollie home, and he could heal up under Grandma's care. It will be rough on Ollie, but we have to catch up to Judith. We'll need all our guns when we catch up to that scum."

Pa nodded. We cut down a couple of young trees and, using our blankets, fashioned a travois. We hooked the travois on Rosie's pack saddle, then loaded it with Ollie and the supplies. We headed out. Fortunately, it hadn't rained for a few days, and we were still able to follow the wagon's track through the grass.

The sun was riding high in the afternoon, beating down hot enough that we all were sweating, men and horses. Ollie finally stirred and moaned. He opened his eyes and looked at the three of us, then in a ragged voice choked out, "Good to see you. Thank God you're here."

Now that Ollie was awake, we stopped for a rest. He was mighty parched and hungry. I held my canteen to his lips, and he drank long and hard. One thing we had was plenty of fresh water, as we were crossing creeks quite often. Then we got some hard tack and jerky into him.

Ollie started talking. "I was out in the barn feeding the team when they hit us. I think they had waited out in the trees until morning. I had the pitchfork in my hands when they rushed into the barn. One of them shot at me with a pistol, but I still got my fork in him. Before I passed out, I heard what sounded like my Springfield being fired in the house. I think Judith must have got a shot off."

After taking another sip of water, Ollie continued, "The sun was high in the western sky when I came to. I knew I'd lost some blood, but being a small calibre, I plugged the hole. I started to follow, but the going was slow. At least I could drink from creeks until I just got wore right down and collapsed. I remember William giving me a drink and then waking up just now."

Looking up at Pa, he carried on, "They're renegade rabble. Some had worn-out Union uniforms, and some had the remains of Reb uniforms. That's all I remember seeing before I blacked out." He fell silent and drifted off to sleep again.

Pa looked over toward Moses and me. "Renegades in mixed uniforms, so scum that was a disgrace to both armies. Probably deserters or released prisoners of war or just plain bad men who have no constraints on them now. There's got to be someone in charge who's tough enough and mean enough to keep close to twenty of these guys in line. He must be promising them something big, or they wouldn't be following him. Judith is in real trouble. We've got to find her. And soon. But where would a gang like this be heading?"

"I been chewin' on that for a while," Moses said, then continued, "East is civilization and law, south is more law, and west is Lakota territory. And they ain't in a good mood these days. Only way is north, Rupert's Land. But why?"

Pa nodded. "That letter I got a while back was from Caleb Daniels, one of my junior officers during the war. He stayed in the army as an intelligence officer. He wanted to know if I would notify him of any groups of men behaving suspiciously and heading north. I guess we're in the middle of something now." Pa paused and then added, almost under his breath, "I hope to God Judith is still alive."

Listening to Pa, I felt a sense of dread. My mind started racing. Why were they taking Judith with them? What had they done with her? I couldn't bear to think of her being hurt.

We had to keep moving, even though we knew it was going to be hell on Ollie. He drifted in and out of consciousness for the rest of the day and that night. We got what food and water we could into him. On the second day, Ollie stayed awake for a couple of hours. No matter how smooth a path we tried to follow, we couldn't avoid hitting some rough patches, and Ollie would groan in pain when the travois hit a bump.

We stopped for a rest in the afternoon. Moses looked down at Ollie while he slept. "I ain't never been to Denmark, but if this feller is an example, they grow 'em mighty tough over there."

I was riding alongside Moses, holding Rosie's shank. Thankfully, she had adapted to the travois. We had hooked her up and put the supplies on it first, and I led her around a bit. After a couple of crow hops and a loud session of braying, she admitted defeat and settled on down. Now she walked along with the travois like she had pulled one for years.

As we rode, Moses was continuing my education. "Jimmy, always keep on the lookout. Anything, and I mean even the tiniest little thing, can mean the difference between living and 'going under.' It might be something as small as a leaf on the ground where it shouldn't be or a bird making a tiny flutter in the trees."

He paused. "These men we're after don't think like you and me. They want something, they take it. And they want it now. If I were the boss man of that bunch, tomorrow—next day at the latest—I would send a few men down my back trail, just to make sure no one is a follerin'. They could set up an ambush and wait. We're far enough behind. We should have three or four days afore we get jumped. Could be a little later. But this man is sharper, meaner, and tougher than the run-of-the-mill scum he's leading."

Pa was riding a little ahead of us when I saw his hand come up. We stopped and got really quiet, and sure enough, we heard the faint squeals of Red River carts.

We turned a little more west, and when we came over a low knoll, we could see three lines of carts coming toward us, a shade over two miles away. Seeing as it was already late in the afternoon, we decided to set up camp for the night at the small stream about a half mile ahead of us. Moses rode on ahead to meet up with the cart brigades.

CHAPTER SIX

In those days, most of the freight from Saint Paul up to Fort Garry—in what was called Rupert's Land—was hauled by these cart brigades. Moses had told me that almost 200 years ago, the King of England gave all the land that drained into the Hudson Bay to the Hudson's Bay Company. Seems the king's cousin Rupert was one of the principal shareholders in the company; hence, the name Rupert's Land. (I had to admit, I was a might confused how the King of England had come to own it in the first place). The Hudson's Bay Company treated this huge piece of land like it was their own little kingdom, only it wasn't so little. Moses had said it was more like the size of the whole United States.

These people made their living hauling freight with the cart brigades. A brigade was ten carts, each pulled by an ox. The ox was tied by a lead rope to the cart ahead of it. This way, ten carts could be managed by four men.

Principally, the cart drivers were Metis people, descended from French voyageurs and Scottish traders who had taken Native wives over the last 200 years. The brigades hauled furs, buffalo hides, and commodities produced on the farms in the area of the Selkirk Settlement and Metis farms along the Red and Assiniboine Rivers—known as the Red River Settlement—south to St. Paul. They then returned north with the carts loaded with manufactured goods needed for the farms and fur trade, such as guns, powder, farm tools, dry goods, and notions needed to make clothing.

Moses knew a fair bit about these people as he had spent half a lifetime amongst them, either trapping in the western mountains, or trading with them since he had settled in Minnesota. Moses once told me that most people didn't realize that over half the trappers in the western mountains were either Metis, French Canadian, or Indians of various eastern tribes, with a lot of them being Iroquois and Delaware.

Moses, like a lot of the old mountain men, could speak enough French to get by, as well as some Indian dialects. Some of the Metis spoke English, so we could find out if they had seen Judith or anything unusual.

Pa and I started to set up our camp. Once I had taken care of the stock and Pa had settled Ollie as comfortably as he could, we commenced to make a shelter.

We were nearly finished when Moses rode up, followed by the cart brigades and their handlers. I gotta tell you, I never saw anything like those fellers making a camp. Seemed to me it was no time at all until the carts were in a big circle and the animals picketed so they could graze.

Ollie, though still in pain, was by now getting almighty hungry again. Moses said it was a good sign. It meant he was going to mend instead of dying of infection or gangrene.

Between ourselves and the freighters, we added our fixings together and came up with a tasty supper. They shared some of their buffalo stew and bannock, and we opened two cans of our peaches. Once everyone had eaten, we commenced to parley with these traders in a mix of French and English, with a smattering of Ojibway and Cree thrown in.

The leader of our new friends was of average height and weight and had the darker complexion of a Metis. He wore a brightly coloured striped sash tied around his waist. He introduced himself as Louis. He did most of the talking and seemed to be able to speak the languages of everybody present.

Moses asked if they had seen a large group of men travelling north. Louis then turned to one of his drivers and spoke to him in what I figured was Cree.

After listening to the man's reply, Louis looked back to Moses and translated, "One Arrow noticed some tracks a couple days back. He was off west of us a mile or so, looking for a deer. He says the tracks were at least a day old, and there was a wagon with them. They were staying close to the trees like they didn't want to be seen."

"Was there any sign of a young woman with them?" Moses asked. "The bastards we're after kidnapped my granddaughter and put a bullet in Ollie here." Then he told the whole story of the events leading up to our meeting, which Louis, in turn, passed along to his men.

Even I, who didn't speak a word of French, Ojibway, or Cree, could tell that didn't go over well with this crowd. There was a lot of parleying going on in four different languages, but I figured out enough to know that if these guys got hold of those renegades and any harm had come to our Judith, it wasn't gonna go good for the kidnappers.

It was now that Pa, looking at Louis, said, "We have another problem. I hate to ask, but would it be possible for you to put Ollie on a cart and go out of your way a few miles? If you could take Ollie to our homestead just off the Woods Trail, my mother could nurse him back to health. We need to catch up with those renegades and get my daughter back. I would be owing you a big debt."

Louis grinned at Pa. "We will gladly do that, monsieur, and you will owe us nothing. Just go get your daughter back."

We turned in not too long after, with Louis telling Moses for us to get some sleep. His men would be standing watch for the night.

We got up before the sun. After a quick breakfast, we saddled up, and the freighters hooked up their carts. When they were ready, we helped load Ollie onto a cart being pulled by one of the biggest oxen I had ever seen. Ollie was awake. He had tears in his eyes as he looked at Pa and said, "Sir, if I could, I would be riding with you. Judith means everything to me." Then his eyes closed in utter exhaustion.

Moses looked down at Ollie and, in a low voice, growled, "We'll get her back, even if we have to track these bastards all the way to the Rocky Mountains."

Just as we were about to leave, Louis approached Moses and spoke in French for a few minutes. When we were mounted, and on our way, Pa looked over at Moses. "So, what did Louis have to say?"

Moses responded, "He was letting me know that things are changing up north. Seems some new directors have taken over the Bay and are now angling to change the whole setup in Rupert's Land. Louis said there's been talk of meetings in the east of uniting Canada with the eastern colonies and forming a country. The new head honchos of the Bay want to start focusing on more settlement and farming, with an end goal of joining Canada. Louis' people may not always be overly fond of the way the Bay runs things up north, but they sure as hell ain't gonna be happy being overrun by a bunch of settlers from the east." Continuing, Moses said, "Add a bunch of American renegades into the mix, and it won't be purdy what happens next."

Pa pondered for a minute or two, then looked at us. "With all of that going on, it would be pretty easy for a gang of Americans to hide out in Rupert's Land, cross south every now and again to raid, and then head back north across the border. They'd be untouchable."

I looked at Pa. "Would that even be possible? Those folks we just met didn't look like the kind of people who would bow down to a small group of renegades. And it could be five years or more before anything changes up there."

Moses nodded to me. "You have a point, Jimmy. But at least now we're pretty sure he's headed north. And with Louis spreading the word, those bastards won't be finding any help from the Metis."

We rode north for a while, angling west of the cart trail. Now, the little groves of trees were getting fewer and farther apart as we were getting closer to the prairie. It was only an hour or so until Pa stopped us. He got off his horse and pointed at the single wagon track in amongst the hoofprints of many horses. "Looks like we've found them." He reached down to a small pile of horse dung and rubbed some between his fingers. "I would say maybe three days at the very most. I'm thinking we've gained at least half a day on them."

We kept on their trail for another two days, only stopping long enough to rest the horses and the mule. We'd make camp late and be riding again before sunup. One camp was a dry one, but that didn't pose a big problem as we always filled our canteens and watered our horses at the streams or small lakes we came across during the day.

And so it was, on the third day after our encounter with the traders, that we found ourselves pinned down in a dry shallow water run with bullets flying over our heads.

Chapter Seven

It was getting to be the hot part of the afternoon, and Pa, Moses, and I were still hunkered down, waiting to see if the bushwhackers would come at us again or cut their losses and run. Then we saw a white flag waving. A scruffy-looking man in the remains of a Confederate uniform came out of the small grove of trees and approached, stopping within 150 yards of us. He hollered out, "Ain't no use anybody else getting hurt. Let's cut a deal. Give us your mule and some rations, and we'll let you fellers go. We're just hungry veterans trying to go home."

Moses murmured to Pa, "They don't have Judith with them. Or they'd be wanting to trade her for the mule and grub."

Pa yelled back to the renegade, "A deal? You bastards took my daughter. Where is she? What have you done with her? Is she even still alive?" He looked at Moses and nodded.

I turned and watched Moses put his hat on his ramrod and start to raise it slowly.

Now, some people just do not know when to shut up and back off. That renegade had to go and lose what little chance he had of coming out of this alive by flapping his gums some more.

"No sirree, we didn't kidnap anybody or shoot no farmer either. Just let us have the…" He never finished.

As Moses's hat started to show above the grass, there was a high-pitched whistle over our heads. That was followed by the whine of a minié ball as more shots erupted from the trees.

Then there was the sharp crack of Pa's carbine. And for the first time in my life, I heard a man scream in mortal agony. Pa had fired fast, aiming to drop the jasper with the flag. His bullet had hit him in the shoulder socket.

Moses looked at Pa. "Let's finish this now. You and Jimmy slide off to the right. I'll go left a ways and keep them distracted enough so you boys can get close. Jimmy, you ready? Remember, take the extra part of a second to aim for the middle of the varmint you're shooting at."

With that, the old man started moving left, and we went right. There was a small creek running within a hundred yards of the trees that the would-be assassins were in. We started crawling on the edge of the creek bank while Moses kept up a steady fire on the trees.

Every few minutes, gunfire erupted from the trees, but they always shot back where Moses had last fired from. With Moses distracting them, we were gaining. We passed by the bodies of the two dead deserters Pa had shot earlier when we had first been ambushed. I have to admit, it didn't bother me in the least. The Good Book said, "Let the Lord cast judgment." I reckoned He could start judging them two a little earlier now.

In the time it took Moses to load and fire his old mountain rifle six times, we'd got to within less than a hundred yards of the trees. "Now, Jimmy," Pa directed, "just raise your carbine long enough to fire a shot into the trees. Drop, reload, and be ready."

I raised my head and carbine just enough to send a round into the trees. I dropped quick, just as two bullets zinged over my head. There was a boom from Moses's old mountain rifle, followed by the sharp crack of Pa's carbine.

Pa and I fired again into the trees to keep the heads down of anyone who might still shoot at Moses. From the trees came a loud cry of someone in pain, then the sound of a horse breaking into a gallop. Moses was already off to the side. That old mountain man had a straightaway shot at a renegade on a running horse. At about 200 yards, the old mountain rifle spoke again, and the rider slowly slid off the horse and crumpled to the ground.

We all dropped in the grass and carefully crawled to the edge of the trees. We waited for what seemed like an eternity but was probably no more than ten minutes. I fired once more, but nothing happened. Pa probed around the little grove for a bit and soon gave the all-clear. I got up and went over to where Pa was standing.

At his feet was a man clutching at a belly wound, obviously not long for this world. Judging by his faded blue pants, he was a deserter from the Union army. Pa stared down at him with pure contempt and demanded, "Where's my daughter? Who are you riding with, and where are you headed? Tell us, and we'll make this easier for you."

"I'm a goner anyway," groaned the wounded bushwhacker.

"Yep, you are," growled Moses, "but it can get a whole lot more painful, and we can make you hurt a whole lot more. That's my granddaughter you bastards took." Looking at Pa and me, Moses jerked his thumb off to his left. "Two more over there a ways. One's dead, the other's unconscious." Then, giving me a wink, he pulled his old Green River and held it against the man's forehead, saying, "Can I scalp this one, William? It lifts off better when they're still alive."

The tough killer started wailing, "No, no, wait! All I ever heard him called is Dixon. He's headed up north and then west. Wants to carve out a large piece of land and make himself the governor or something. He says there is no real law up there and nobody to stop him. Says the injuns is more peaceable up there. We was foraging and stopped at a farm. Some of the boys was gonna have a good time with this blonde-haired gal, and she shot one of us. Then Dixon came into the cabin and said she was his. I really don't know all his plans," whined the outlaw. He begged, "Please don't scalp me 'til after I'm dead."

Moses looked down at the dying creature at his feet with disgust. "Not scalping you anyways. Don't need anything to remind me of you. You're nothing but scavenger food."

Pa glanced at me. "Let's check on the other two here and then see if the guy who had the white flag is still kicking."

Moses led us over to where the other two bushwhackers were laying. One was definitely dead, blood from the wound in the middle of his chest staining his filthy and faded Union blue shirt. The second one was another matter. This one was wearing the remains of a ragged Confederate uniform. His leg was shattered below the knee. He desperately tried to get up when he saw us but collapsed back to the ground. He moaned in pain, looking up at Pa, begging, "For God's sake, help me!"

Pa glared down at him. "You kidnap my daughter, shoot my son-in-law, try to kill us, and you want help? You'd better be giving us some information on the rest of your outfit. How many men does this Dixon have with him?"

The wounded man pleaded, almost crying, "He'll kill me if I talk. I've seen what he's done to others."

"Well, sonny, I will kill you real slow if you don't talk. Real slow and painful," growled Moses.

"We picked up a few more men, and he's got over twenty with him now. He's promising all of us a bunch of money when we get up north. Even more are supposed to meet up with him past Fort Garry somewhere," sobbed the pathetic outlaw.

"Why would Dixon take my daughter?"

"Dixon seen her and said she was the prettiest thing he'd ever laid eyes on. And so—he took her. You don't know this guy. If he wants something, he just takes it. And you don't question him. If you wanna live—you obey," he wailed.

Pa looked down at the ground at the rifle with a telescope mounted on the side. "Is this your Whitworth?"

"No," groaned the wounded gunman. "It was my brother's. After he got killed at North Anna, the captain gave it to me, but I was never very good with it."

While Pa was grilling the bushwhacker, Moses and I headed back to check on the one Pa had shot in the shoulder. He was dead. Pa's .50-calibre bullet had shattered his shoulder, and he'd bled out. Then we walked out to the one Moses had shot off his horse. He was also dead, lung shot.

We hiked back to Pa in time to see him throwing a rope over a good stout tree limb.

The wounded deserter wailed up to Moses, "You said you'd kill me if I didn't talk. Well, I told you everything I know."

"I said I would kill you real slow if you didn't talk. Hanging ain't slow. You and the rest of your kind were dead men walking the minute you took my granddaughter."

The gutshot one had expired by the time we hung the wounded outlaw. We gathered up their guns and horses. It was getting toward evening, but we caught our horses and Rosie and travelled a couple of hours before we made camp. We wanted to get some miles between us and all the death. We knew it could just as easily have been our carcasses the buzzards and crows were picking at.

The more I heard about this Dixon, the more worried I got for Judith. Judith had never been one to give up easily, ever since she was a little girl. And she had managed to kill one of her attackers at the farm. I just hoped she could hang on until we got to her.

CHAPTER EIGHT

We had one more day of good tracking, and then the rain hit. Not a drizzle either, but a good old-fashioned gully-washing downpour!

We had seen it moving in all day, so late in the afternoon, we stopped at a grove of trees and threw a shelter together as quickly as we could. With the ground sheets and ponchos of the dead deserters, we made a lean-to big enough for the three of us and our supplies. We had just enough time to gather wood for a good fire.

It rained hard for two days. One of us would go out and move the picket line for the horses every few hours, but the rest of the time, we hunkered down in our shelter. We used the time to clean all the guns, including the ones we had taken from our would-be killers. We had acquired six rifled muskets (two Springfield, three Enfield, and one Austrian Lorentz), an 1842 Springfield .69-calibre smoothbore, the Whitworth sniper rifle with a scope and bullet mould, and a .36-calibre Whitney Navy revolver, which Pa said was one of the better pistols made.

Pa looked at Moses and asked, "Any of this hardware catch your eye?"

"Yep," Moses answered. "I want that smoothbore. We can get the barrel and stock cut down to about twenty inches. Loaded with eight or ten .36-calibre pistol balls, that old girl will cut quite a swath."

"You don't want the revolver?" questioned Pa.

"I was in a lot of fights in the mountains with my rifle, pistol, tomahawk, and my Green River. Give that six-shooter to Jimmy."

There was an army holster with a flap, so the pistol didn't bounce out when riding. I buckled on the holster and figured it fit fairly decent.

Digging through the saddle bags we had acquired, we found a .36-calibre bullet mould and some paper cartridges for the pistol. Rummaging some more, Pa also found some paper cartridges for the Whitworth, which meant we could use the sniper rifle if we had to make a long shot someday.

We hashed over our various ideas of what to do now, seeing as this rain had taken care of any tracks we could have followed. The only thing we could come up with was that we would have to ride to Fort Garry and the surrounding settlements. These fellers we were after might be a bunch of killers and kidnappers, but they would still need supplies.

The sun came out the next morning, and we headed north to the border, making good time as we didn't have to burn daylight looking for tracks. As we travelled, we would take a few minutes each morning for me to fire a few shots with the pistol. Pa would set up a couple of pieces of wood at about twenty yards for targets. I remember him always saying, "Draw your gun deliberately. Don't try for a fast draw; be the most accurate shooter. Always aim for the middle of your target and never try to wound him. Trying to wound will get you killed if you miss."

After a few shots with the Whitney, I had it figured out. While I might never be a fast draw, I usually hit what I aimed for. Now, I don't know of anyone who wants to shoot anybody, other than the killers we shot, but there are times when you gotta do what you gotta do. I had made up my mind that if I had to kill someone to get my sister back, so be it. As far as Moses, Pa, and I were concerned, anyone involved in Ollie's shooting and Judith's kidnapping was on borrowed time. We were bringing her *home*!

On the ninth day after leaving Grandma, we crossed the border. Moses told me that it had finally been surveyed and marked by 1863. Wherever there were trees, the border had been marked with a twenty-foot slash. In the eastern parts, where there were lots of trees, this worked fine. Out on the prairie, where we crossed, there was no visible marker, but by midafternoon, Moses figured we were in Rupert's Land. By now, we were following the Red River north. We made camp on the high ground off the riverbank—high ground being defined rather liberally.

We had some willows for shelter, and it didn't rain, so we could rest. Tomorrow we would be running into settlements and probably more carts. Our conversation was rather muted while we made camp and had our supper. It was the not knowing if my sister was even still alive that was weighing heavy on us that night.

I cleaned the Whitney by firelight after supper. Moses and Pa cast some more pistol balls for me, and some more bullets for the Whitworth. We turned in early, hoping to catch a break somehow tomorrow.

By the time the sun was peaking over the horizon, we had all the horses saddled, Rosie packed up, and we were on the trail north. The countryside was fairly flat prairie. As we got closer to the settlement, we could see fields of grain reaching back from the river.

We rode into a small parish town at midmorning. It wasn't a very big settlement—a few frame houses, a fairly decent-sized white Catholic church, a little general store, and a blacksmith. We rode up to the blacksmith—a big man with a leather apron and his shirt sleeves rolled up. Even though it was only midmorning, between the mugginess after the rain and the heat from his forge, he had already worked up quite a sweat. After exchanging pleasantries, Moses got off his horse and started to parley in French. After a few minutes, he went to the horse carrying the smoothbore and took the musket over to the blacksmith.

While the blacksmith was cutting down the barrel and stock, Moses had time to update us on what he had learned from the man.

He started by nodding over at the blacksmith as he was putting the gun in a vise. "He says three rough-looking characters came through here four days ago asking about some other riders they were looking to meet up with. His brother's the storekeeper, and he said they picked up a lot of grub for three guys, and even bought soap. He figured that was kind of odd as they didn't look like the type to wash too often. Also said there have been some strange happenings...some gardens having a few things missing, a little oats gone at a couple of farms. Not a lot, but like someone trying to sneak through without being noticed or not being a big enough bother for folks to ask around much."

"That soap's for Judith. These guys are part of the main group, probably asking about the trash we put under," Pa surmised. "Four days. Damn it, we're not gaining on them."

"Pa, what if they holed up somewhere for a day or two, waiting for those dead bushwhackers? We might be a whole day closer than you're thinking." I had been doing some figuring on this while Moses was talking to the blacksmith.

"Jimmy might be right, William. We can't count on it, but it might be so. Our best bet is to get up to Fort Garry and ask around," Moses commented before turning to the blacksmith who had walked up with the sawed-off musket. Moses went to pay the man, who shook his head. He spoke in French for a few minutes and then returned to work.

Moses looked at Pa and me, saying, "He won't take anything for cutting down the musket. I had told him about Judith earlier, and he figures we would be doing the settlements a favour if we shoot the whole pack of them varmints."

Pa and I both nodded to the man in thanks, and we headed out to the fort.

The sun was due west as we looked across the Red River toward Fort Garry. We could see a ferry approaching us. A passing local had told us about what we could expect.

As it came up to the shore, we looked at the dilapidated scow as water washed over the floorboards. The side rails even looked rickety. "At least we can all swim if it sinks," commented Moses.

"I hope it has a couple of crossings left in it," I wondered out loud.

"I've seen worse. Mind you, they were sitting on shore," laughed Pa. "We just as well start. I will take the spare horses across first, then you guys cross with ours."

Pa went down and paid the ferry operator, who looked about as well kept as his vessel. Then we loaded Pa with the extra horses, and he was on his way.

We followed on the next trip across. Moses looked at me. "I think next time we cross this river, we'll be lookin' for a ford. I ain't never been in a shipwreck yet, and I don't plan on bein' in one."

I laughed nervously as the scow bobbed a bit, and we took on about twenty gallons of water. "We ain't all the way across yet!"

However, the old ferry did deliver us to where Pa was waiting. He'd asked the ferryman if any rough-looking, well-armed men had crossed lately. But other than locals, no one like that had been by the past week.

We mounted and rode up to the fort. Now this was the biggest fort I had ever seen. I remember a small fur trading post we had stopped at when I was a young boy. It had just been some log walls and some small log buildings. This place was massive, with stone walls fifteen feet high!

We went into the fort through a gate in the middle of the south wall. My lord, this place was big. And busy! There were people everywhere we looked. Even Pa, who had been in some of the big cities in the east, commented that there were a lot of people here. We could see at least two brigades of freighters unloading their carts in front of warehouses, their oxen patiently swishing at flies with their tails. Some Native trappers were leading a couple of pack horses loaded down with furs. A few farmers had just finished unloading their wagonloads of hay at the livery stable. At the far end of the fort, we could see a huge white house.

Fortunately for us, the days were long this time of year, so when we finally found the general store in the southwest corner of the fort, it was still open for business. We stepped inside and looked around. There were shelves upon shelves filled with dry goods, blankets, clothing, tools, traps for hunting, trade muskets and ammunition, harnesses, and all manner of farm supplies.

"I'm Charles Affleck. What can I do for you gents?" asked the storekeeper with a hint of Scotland in his voice.

Pa introduced us and commenced to tell the storekeeper of our hunt for Judith.

The storekeeper shook his head sadly, saying, "I'm sorry, I'm afraid we haven't seen any sign of your daughter." He then called a young Native, who looked to be three or four years younger than me, over to the counter. He quickly wrote a note and handed it to the lad, telling him, "Take this to the governor's residence and wait for a reply."

Then looking back to us, he asked, "Is there anything else I could help you with?"

"Well, we have some rifled muskets, saddles, and horses to trade or sell," Pa replied.

"I'll take a look at the rifle muskets first. I imagine we'll be seeing more of them in the next few years, as yon war is finally over." Aflleck inspected the guns closely, asking various questions about them, such as if we had cartridges or bullet moulds for them.

We had about a hundred and twenty cartridges for the six rifles. Cartridges for the rifle muskets consisted of a minié bullet wrapped in greased paper with the powder charge. A soldier would bite off the end of the paper cartridge, pour the powder down the barrel, and then ram the bullet down. The bullet was slightly smaller than the barrel, so it could still be loaded reasonably fast, even when the gun was fouled by black powder from the previous shots. What made the guns accurate was that the bullet had a hollow base that expanded into the rifling grooves of the barrel when fired.

Mr. Affleck then turned his attention to the saddles. "I'll tell you what—leave the guns and the saddles here, and I'll give you an offer in the morning. I know a local fella that will board your horses in his stable, and we can maybe make a deal on the ones you want to sell."

About then was when the messenger returned and handed the merchant a note. He nodded, saying, "I thought the governor would be interested. MacTavish would like to meet with you at your soonest convenience. I can have your horses looked after now if you would like to go up to the governor's residence. It's the big house at the far end of the fort."

Leaving the store, we made our way through the fortress to the governor's house. Things had slowed down now that evening was approaching, and there wasn't nearly the amount of activity that there had been an hour ago.

"What a place," Moses marvelled aloud. "Had a Bay man tell me about the original Fort Garry back when I was in the mountains. Man, it wasn't nothin' this big."

"The way I remember," Pa added, "that was farther north, closer to a big lake that was almost as big as some of the great lakes."

By now, we were at the door of what Pa called a mansion. I knocked, and it was shortly opened by a young man. "You must be the Munros. My uncle is in the dining room. We took the liberty of assuming you might be hungry, so come on in and have some supper."

He led the way into a large dining room that was warmly lit with kerosene lanterns. There was a table covered with a linen cloth, long enough to seat twenty people. There were three place settings waiting for us. At the head of the table sat a man of around fifty years of age with a thick head of hair and a full beard. He had the look of a man given a great deal of responsibility, and it was starting to weigh heavily.

"Sit down, gentlemen. I'm William MacTavish, Governor of the Red River Colony and Governor of Rupert's Land." He indicated heaped plates containing buffalo steak, fresh bread, potatoes, gravy, and a variety of fresh vegetables. "Please help yourselves to some food. And then you can tell me what has brought you here and why you have spare horses and American guns to sell."

"Thank you," Pa answered. "We're most grateful, sir. I guess if you figured we were outlaws, you'd have already arrested us."

Between the three of us, we commenced to tell our host the entire story of our situation up until now. I will say this for the governor: he was a good listener. He never once interrupted us while we were telling our tale.

Waiting until we were finished, he looked at us and then said, "Now I will tell you a story. The Hudson Bay Company was formed almost two hundred years ago, with a monopoly on the fur trade in all the lands draining into Hudson Bay. No one at the time knew how big an area that would be. Competition would come along from Americans out in the Oregon Country and from various companies that were formed in Montreal. To make the story short and simple, the companies out of Montreal merged into one company, The Northwest Company. Competition was fierce, bordering on warfare at times. Under pressure from the British government, the companies were made to merge in 1821.

"In 1811, the first settlers for the Selkirk Colony arrived. It was tough for a lot of years, what with cold winters, drought, locusts, and company politics. It is a wonder the colony survived, but it did."

Looking at us, he continued, "Just as things are starting to look like we might finally have some stability around here, the Canadian colonies are talking of merging into a dominion, basically becoming a country of their own. They haven't even joined together yet, and they have agitators here, wanting Canada to take over this area as well. We've had an influx of settlers from Upper Canada, and they are quite vocal about what they want."

He sighed. "Now you are telling me I've got a batch of American renegades, armed to the teeth, taking what they want, riding around up here. What a mess.

"Gentlemen, it's getting late, and I am tired. Shall we continue in the morning? I have plenty of rooms in this house. My nephew will show you where you can sleep, and we will take this up again after a good night's rest." With that, the governor rose and left the room.

We were shown to our rooms. I laid down but wasn't able to get to sleep. My mind kept going back over all the governor had told us at supper. I couldn't help but wonder if all that was happening up here might impact us while we were trying to find Judith. I eventually drifted off into a troubled sleep.

CHAPTER NINE

In the morning, we were up before sunrise. We walked quietly downstairs, only to be surprised by the governor already up. He was pouring himself a cup of tea from a silver teapot. Looking up at us, he asked, "Tea or coffee? I've got both."

While we were pouring our morning brew, his housekeeper bustled into the dining room, bearing plates of bacon, eggs, and biscuits. She set them on the table and then brought in pots of jam and honey. Man, I could get used to eating like this!

After we'd polished off every last speck of grub on that table, the governor began to speak. "I've given considerable thought to this." Looking at Moses, he asked, "Could you swear to be loyal to the queen while in the colony and Rupert's Land? As governor, I can grant you a special commission to hunt down these people you are after and recover your Judith. They will not be giving up easily. If you must kill some of these scoundrels to get your girl back, it's best that we make it as legal as we can. Also, without a doubt, they will be trouble for the colony in the unsettled times ahead."

Surveying all three of us with his gaze, he continued, "I don't know how things will play out here in Rupert's Land, but I have a feeling that, when the dust settles, the colonies and the West will all be part of Canada. My wife is Metis, and I see nothing good coming out of this for her people. I know there are those in the British government who want the Bay to sell out to Canada. I strongly suspect that I will be the last Governor of Rupert's Land, and it will spell the end of a way of life for a lot of people. Even so, we don't need a power-hungry American in our midst, with his own small army. What say you, gentlemen?"

And so it was that all three of us were sworn in as special constables for the Red River Colony and Rupert's Land, our commissions signed by Governor William MacTavish himself. He asked Pa and Moses if we needed more men with us. Pa declined, saying, "We can move more quickly and quietly on our own. But if we could get some fresh horses, more ammunition, and top up our trail rations, that would be greatly appreciated."

"Certainly. I'll write up a note for you to take to Mr. Affleck at the store." Then, wishing us good hunting, MacTavish shook our hands. "Something else to keep in mind, gentlemen. There is a gold rush happening in the mountains, which might be tempting to this Dixon. We've already seen some wagons of prospectors pass through here earlier this summer." With that said, he rose from the table and headed into his office to carry on the business of his dual responsibilities.

We departed from the mansion and started our hike over to the general store.

"You know, I had a grandfather who fought against King George in the War of Independence. And now I'm swearing to uphold the laws of Queen Victoria herself! Don't that beat all you ever seen?" Moses marvelled aloud.

"'The enemy of my enemy is my friend,'" quoted Pa.

"Guess he is at that," sighed Moses. "If it helps us bring Judith home, it's worth it."

Even this early in the morning, there was already a lot of activity in the fort. We saw a cart brigade ahead, just about ready to pull out. Pa and Moses looked at each other, and Pa said, "We need to start asking around. Somebody, somewhere, has seen something that's out of place. What do you think of talking to that freight outfit? Jimmy and I will go in the general store, do some business, and ask around."

"I'll see what I can find out. We gotta have an idea where to head when we leave," replied Moses before he wandered over to the carts.

Pa and I made our way to the store. We were constantly looking over every person in sight. In this mass of people, there had to be someone who knew something that could help us find Judith. It was a possibility that one of Dixon's men was here even now, on the lookout for us. If that were the case, it occurred to me that we would have a problem.

"Pa, what if they've got someone in the fort keeping an eye on things for this Dixon?"

"I'm betting he does, Jimmy. He has undoubtedly realized that something must have happened to the men he sent back to see if he was being followed. He will be getting suspicious, and he's sharp enough to be gathering intelligence. We arrived here yesterday with eight extra horses and some rifled muskets to sell. If he didn't already know we're after him, he will now." Pa continued, "The problem is, what is he going to do about it? Try to kill us right here in the fort? Could be done, but it would have to look like self-defense."

"Pa," I asked, "What if they spread around a story that we are the killers, and we murdered the owners of the horses? Even if it created doubt in just a few people, it would sure make things more difficult for us."

"You might have something there, Jimmy. Let's see if maybe we can nip that scenario in the bud before it happens."

Now, it looked to us that the busiest place in the entire fort was the general store. If there was going to be a clearing house for news, this was it. Entering the store, we could see some traders and farmers were already in there. When they saw us, they eyed us with suspicion, and things got real quiet real fast.

"They've already been spreading their lies," Pa whispered to me. Then he raised his voice. "I am Captain William Munro, formerly of the US Army." Reaching into his pocket, he pulled out the commission from Governor MacTavish. He showed it to the storekeeper and a few others.

"I suspect someone has been in here this morning, spreading rumours about how we acquired the extra horses and rifles we had for trade. The truth is, we were ambushed a few days ago and managed to come out of it on top. These men were with the outfit that kidnapped my daughter, Judith, and shot my son-in-law, Ollie Johansen. My father, Moses Munro, and my son, Jimmy Munro, also hold special constable commissions." Pa looked over the group and continued, "Any information would be appreciated—anything you've noticed out of the ordinary. The ones who ambushed us were wearing remains of uniforms from the recent hostilities to the south."

Then he went handed the storekeeper the note from Governor MacTavish, authorizing fresh horses and supplies. The storekeeper looked up at Pa. "There was a clean-looking fella in here earlier this morning. He wanted to buy the guns. But seeing as you stayed at the governor's house last night, I was pretty sure you were on the up and up. I overheard him trying to get folks worked up against you. I will do all I can to help your cause, but just know there will still be a few who will wonder."

"What did he look like?" Pa asked.

"About your height. Big in the shoulders, dark hair. Carries himself like he owns the place. You can't miss him. I've never seen this before, but he had one blue eye and one brown eye."

Pa looked at me and then replied, "Thank you. That helps us a lot. We should be able to recognize at least this guy if we come across him. It's more information than we had."

Then Pa and Mr. Affleck got down to haggling over the horses, saddles, and guns we had left the night before.

That storekeeper may have believed us—even liked us—but that didn't stop him from driving a hard bargain. Pa did manage to get sixty Yankee dollars each for the horses, fifteen dollars each for the saddles, and five dollars and fifty cents each for the rifled muskets. We had to throw in the bridles with the saddles and the paper cartridges for the muskets. We came out of that with a grand total of four hundred and fifty-three dollars.

Then, as authorized by the governor, we got powder for Moses's rifle and all our pistols, balls (in all three calibres), and some buckshot and felt wadding for the smoothbore. Percussion caps for all our guns were also a must. We weren't looking for a war, but we were pretty sure one was coming to us.

We also loaded up on rations courtesy of the governor: dried fruit, hard tack, bacon, flour, fresh apples, and some airtights of peaches. We bought some pemmican as well. As I recall, there was a lot of it on hand.

By the time Pa bought more goods to have on hand so that we had extra to trade with on the trail, we were down to less than four hundred dollars.

We had just left the store when Moses came striding back through the fort's main gate. Moses grinned at us. "Our girl is still alive!"

Pa exclaimed, "Thank God!" as I jumped up and let out a war whoop of joy.

Moses went on to tell us what he had found out. "No one in the fort that I talked to had seen anything that would help our cause. So I went for a walk outside the fort walls. I hit pay dirt, boys! I ran into an Iroquois feller who just got here early yesterday. He had been trading out west and had travelled here on what the locals call the Carlton Trail. Said he wandered off the trail a ways a couple days ago, looking for some fresh meat. He figured he was about half an hour north of the trail when he seen a wagon track in amongst the tracks of around thirty shod horses. Out of curiosity, he followed the tracks for a couple miles and then found a campsite he estimated was three days old. Boys, they had camped by a small lake, and in a little patch of sandy shore, someone had made a 'J' with their finger! It has to be our Judith, leaving us a sign."

We didn't waste any time. We went right over to the livery stable and showed them Governor MacTavish's authorization. When we were done swapping out our own saddle horses and Rosie plus the three horses we had kept for ourselves from the bushwhackers, we now had seven fresh mounts. We planned on rotating the horses so we could make better time, and Pa put Rosie's pack saddle on one of the spare horses.

In less than half an hour, we were on our way toward Fort Carlton. We figured we could gain on Judith's kidnappers on the trail. And there would be enough cart traffic that we might be able to find out more information on the way.

Once we were on the trail, Moses started telling us more of what he had learned from talking to various traders and cart drivers. "Seems the Lakota are all stirred up south of the line. Gold has been found between the Madison and Jefferson Rivers. If I'm remembering right, I trapped on the Jefferson back in '28. Guess that country is ruined now."

"Would Dixon be headed there?" I asked.

"I sure hope not," Pa answered. "He would be crazy to try. There are hundreds of hostile Lakota, the Blackfoot won't be happy seeing him and his crowd, and they won't be trusted by any other tribe they run into."

"They'll likely stay in this country," Moses surmised. "By and large, the tribes up here in the west haven't lost any land to white men. It's coming, but it hasn't happened yet. Then you will see a fight. But for now, I don't see any fighting until the Canadians start pouring in here and grabbing land."

Looking at me, he said, "Water flows, Jimmy. So do people. While water flows downhill, people flow from where they are crowded to where it's not crowded. Mark my words, this will be all settled in fifty or sixty years, and the tribes will be on reservations. Just like Uncle Sam is doing at home."

As he spoke, it saddened me to realize that an entire way of life was going to disappear in my lifetime. Looking back, I don't think any of the tribes or the Metis could have fathomed in how short a span of time Rupert's Land would be forever changed.

Now, we were covering ground: getting up early, riding for a few hours, stopping to rest the horses, letting them graze a bit, fixing us some grub, swapping a couple of saddles, and getting back on the trail.

If it didn't rain, we would be able to follow the tracks of the wagon and riders fairly easily. At the rate we were pushing the horses, we were gaining, but our horses were going to need a rest soon. If possible, we were hoping to swap for some fresh horses at Fort Ellice, which, by the amount of ground we were covering, would be a long four-day ride. At least the trail we were following ran through country that had plenty of water. Pa and Moses told me this might not be the case if we had to go south and west from the Qu'Appelle Valley.

Moses had spent many years trapping in the mountains. He had a reasonable understanding of the lay of the land where we were headed, from talking with other traders and trappers who had passed through these parts at one time or another. We were taking turns riding point. One of us would ride ahead for a few miles while the other two would follow up with the pack animal and the spare riding horses.

On the morning of the fourth day since leaving Fort Garry, it was my turn to be out in front. I was riding about a mile ahead when I smelled smoke. I stopped and looked around. It wasn't what you would call breezy, but there was a little air movement from the southwest. I sniffed the air for a minute or two. I have been around wood smoke and burning brush all my life, but this was different. There was the smell of burnt wood mixed with the stench of rotting, charred flesh. The unmistakable smell of death. I immediately flashed back to the scene at Judith and Ollie's cabin and hoped with all my might that it wasn't Judith's body we'd find ahead of us.

I quickly raised my carbine above my head three times, signalling Pa and Moses.

Leading the spare horses, they trotted up beside me in a few minutes. As they got closer, I heard Moses mutter, "Oh, Lord. I remember that smell all too well."

Pa looked at me grimly, a haunted look on his face. "I smelled that so many times during the war. The stench hung over a battlefield for weeks… burnt wagons, dead bodies of men and livestock. I'd hoped to never smell that again."

Pa motioned. "We'll have a look. I pray it isn't Judith. Let's stay to the trees and work our way up slow. Could be another ambush. Or just some poor freighters who wanted a break from the trail and had found a nice place to rest… right in the path of these renegades."

Once we got to the crest of the hill, we split up and slowly worked our way through the scattered brush and trees. I was on the left, where the going was a little easier, and after working my way slowly down the hill, I came to the edge of the brush and could see the carnage.

In front of me were the burnt-out remains of three Red River carts. The oxen had been roughly butchered, the remains covered with flies and maggots. The stench was unbearable. Surveying the scene before me, I swallowed hard to keep down the bile that was rising in my throat.

About then, Moses and Pa came into the camp from their respective sides. "The murdering bastards," Moses swore.

There before us were two dead men wearing the distinctive red sashes of the Metis. One had thinning grey hair; the other appeared to be younger, with jet-black hair. It looked like they had been taken completely unawares. Both had been shot in the back and were lying face down in the dirt by their campfire. Death had been quick for both.

Pa had started walking around the camp in ever larger circles. He was just on the edge of the brush when he hollered, "Over here!"

Moses and I hurried to where he was. There was another body, this one a middle-aged woman. Her calico dress was dark with dried blood. It looked like she had tried to escape after the other two men had been shot. She had almost made her way into the brush before she had been cut down in a hail of bullets.

In absolute disgust, I blurted out, "What kind of men are these? It's bad enough that they killed the men in such a cowardly way. But to shoot a woman like this?"

Pa grimly declared, "If there were ever men that deserved to be shot and burn in hell, it's surely this bunch."

"Amen to that," Moses agreed.

There was nothing more we could do for these poor souls except to give them as good a burial as we could. I found a shovel in the remains of one of the carts. The handle was burnt off, but it wasn't hard to fashion one from a young tree.

While Pa and I dug three shallow graves, Moses went on a scout for any sign he could find. By the time we had the graves ready, he had returned.

"Boys, we're on the right track. Judith managed to leave us another sign! I rode around for a bit, figurin' there must be water not too far away from these folks' camp, and I came across a pond. It looks to me like whoever is the head honcho of this outfit lets Judith wash away from the rest of the riffraff. Our girl was smart enough to take advantage of that and left us another marker in the sand by the edge of the water." He bent down and, in the closest pile of dirt, wrote with his finger, J + 1.

He looked solemnly at me and Pa. "They got another girl."

Then we buried the cart people. Pa, who had seen more men buried than I'd ever want to imagine, said some words over these folks, and we got back on the trail.

Chapter Ten

We had lost some time, so it wasn't until the next day that the buildings of Fort Ellice came into view. This fort wasn't the huge stone monstrosity of Fort Garry. It was more in line with what comes to mind of a frontier fort—a wooden palisade with warehouses and storage sheds for trade goods, built on the confluence of the Qu'Appelle and the Assiniboine Rivers.

We rode through the gate and were just inside when suddenly we were surrounded by men with guns pointed at us. They didn't look very happy to see us, and I could see one of them carrying some rope.

That's when Pa yelled, "Hold up. You've got the wrong guys! The killers are ahead of us. I am Captain William Munro. I am going to reach into my coat pocket and pull out my commission, signed by Governor William MacTavish himself. We are special constables of the Red River Colony and for Rupert's Land."

An older man with a trade musket pointed at Pa spoke up. "Okay, laddie, show us. Real slow."

Pa carefully pulled out his commission and unfolded it. The old Scotsman took the paper and looked at it. After some consideration, he turned to the small crowd of men and said, "Put the guns down, lads. It's MacTavish's signature, all right."

Looking up at Pa, he explained, "Sorry, Captain Munro, but we had a couple of fellows pass through here three days ago, saying there were three killers on the loose. Of course, they gave your description. Those would be the men you are after, I take it?"

"They are. And I guess this proves they had someone on the lookout at Fort Garry for us," Pa agreed. "They're a bunch of renegade deserters from both armies in our recent hostilities south of the border. They kidnapped my daughter and shot my son-in-law. Now we fear they have another girl, as well." Looking around, Pa asked, "Was there a small group with three carts through here recently? A grey-haired man, middle-aged woman, and a younger man with black hair? And possibly a younger woman?"

One trader spoke up. "Marcel Fournier left here four days ago, heading east. His wife, son, and daughter were with him. They were going back to the settlements for the winter after spending the summer hunting and trading out west."

Looking at the man, Pa could only say, "I'm sorry. I'm afraid they met up with the men we are after. We found three bodies by the burnt-out carts, and the oxen had all been butchered. From the message my daughter managed to leave for us in the sand, we suspect they abducted the daughter and are holding her along with our Judith. We buried them as best we could, and I said a few words over them."

The Scotsman spoke again. "Captain Munro, I'm the assistant factor here, name's McCrimmon. I'll send some men to bring Marcel's family back here for a Christian burial. I'm shorthanded right now as it is, so I can only spare you a couple of men to augment your force."

"Well, Mr. McCrimmon, I appreciate your offer. But unless they're experienced fighters, I think you'd best keep your men here. We're gaining on these men, and our small group is best for following," Pa responded. "We could use some fresh horses, though."

"That we can do. We can swap out your six riding horses. You can pick up your own horses on your way home. You've got a long, hard ride ahead to catch those renegades." McCrimmon continued, "The next fort on the trail is Qu'Appelle. An outfit as big as you're saying will be needing supplies."

McCrimmon then asked, "Are you aware that there is gold in the western mountains? A group of people left Fort Garry in '62. I've been told they made it to the gold fields, but they left Garry in early June. It's already mid-August, and it sounds like this bunch you're after are greenhorns to this country. If that is where they are headed, you'd better rescue your girl before they get to the mountains. They'd need a guide, and nobody that's any good would even try this late. It'd be mid-October when they get to the mountain passes. It would be another Donner Party affair.

"We had five wagons pass through here a few weeks ago. I tried to tell them to winter back in Garry and head out earlier next year, but they had gold fever. They were going to follow the trail all the way to Fort Edmonton and continue through the Yellowhead to Barkerville. I wouldn't give them a snowball's chance in hell, but you know how it is—gold fever will make fools out of sensible people."

Pa thanked McCrimmon for the horses and the advice. With the traders helping us switch packs and catch horses, we were ready to head out again in less than half an hour. As we mounted up and started for the gate, Moses looked down at McCrimmon and the crowd, cautioning, "If any of these people we're huntin' show up here, be careful. They kill to get what they want, and they don't give any warning."

With that, we were back on the chase. We angled off the trail for close to an hour before we regained the tracks of our kidnappers. It looked to us like they were still almost three days ahead. We had to ride hard and cover ground if we were going to catch them.

Chapter Eleven

We were having a break from the heat of the midafternoon, resting the horses. I started thinking out loud. "Pa, by now, this Dixon knows we took care of the eight guys he sent to watch his back trail. What if he sends back an even larger group of men to hit us? We might get some of them, but for sure, they'd get all of us."

"I've been pondering on that too," Pa answered. "That and the nagging problem of still not knowing what are they up here for. The most likely thing I can think of after hearing of the gold is that they are headed to the mountains."

"They're pilgrims to the mountains," chimed in Moses. "We have to get our girl back before she's part of another Donner Party affair."

"I've heard of the Donner Party but not much of what really happened. Who were they?" I questioned Moses.

Moses started talking slow, looking off to the horizon. "Me and your Pa were scouting on the Oregon Trail in the summer and fall of '46. We had taken a wagon train through to the Oregon Country and were riding back to Independence. We were the first train of the season and had gotten our people to Oregon in four and a half months.

"We had left your grandma with your mother and baby Judith at home, so we were quite happy to be headed back earlier than we'd planned. We ran into a late group of immigrants at Fort Hall on the Snake River. They had got a late start, but I later heard they made it to California with no more hardship than anybody else."

Moses got quiet, and Pa took up the story. "See, west of Fort Hall, the trail split—northwest to Oregon, southwest to California. We met these folks, shared a meal, and never saw them again. Like Moses said, they made it. But they told us that when they came through Fort Bridger, some of their original group got talked into taking some new trail. A fellow, name of Hastings, said it was a shortcut. George Donner had been elected the leader of this group, and they set out to go south through a desert and some rugged mountain trails. They finally rejoined the trail to California, but by then, it was too late in the season. They got caught in a snowstorm in the high mountains in early November and couldn't move. The ones who made it through the winter did so by eating all the stock. And when that ran out, they ate the dead people. The survivors were rescued after four months. A little over half of the eighty-seven people on those wagons lived to see California."

I gulped. Eating dead people to survive? I could never have imagined anything so awful.

Moses spoke up again. "We've got to get Judith back, and soon. We do *not* want her near those mountains. The

Rockies up here make the mountains farther south look like hills, and they will be even colder."

We remounted and got back on the trail, one of us scouting ahead and the other two coming along behind with the packs and extra horses.

All of us had the gut feeling that something was about to happen, but what and when? And we now had to consider that there was another girl who could not be left with these renegades.

We really had to determine where this Dixon was headed. Would they leave the cart trail and head off on their own into the wilderness, or stay on course? The only way to the gold fields, as far as we knew, was through Fort Edmonton. Right now, they were moving in the direction of Fort Qu'Appelle. Would they head north to Edmonton? That could take at least six weeks, probably more, and if they had a good scout, he would know it was too late to try to get through the mountains. They would need a place to hunker down until next spring. If they were on their own, without a scout, it was all up for grabs—anything could happen. Or was this Dixon feller after a piece of land to set up his own little kingdom? Either way, something had to break real soon.

We figured we had two days yet to get to Fort Qu'Appelle when Pa called for a break to rest the horses. Once we had dismounted and loosened cinches, he started talking. "I do not like this one little bit. If it were me in this Dixon's boots, by now, I'd have sent back enough men to hit us hard and take us out, so I wasn't looking back over my shoulder all the time."

"You got that right," Moses agreed. "Remember back when those Rees stole some of our horses back in '38? You were about Jimmy's age. It was the first time I took you with me to the mountains. We followed those horse thieves for five days. Then we started gaining on them, and something didn't feel right. That night, we filled our bed rolls with brush and hid in the trees. Sure enough, some of them had doubled back and snuck into our camp after midnight. We were ready for them, and we sent all three of them to meet their maker."

Pa looked at me. "The more I think about it, if I was Dixon, I would go for a night attack. Tonight would be best because we're still a couple days out of Fort Qu'Appelle. The farther from the fort, the less chance of our bodies being found soon. Tomorrow night would be his last chance until after Qu'Appelle. Jimmy, we've got to be prepared for an attack."

I gritted my teeth and nodded, saying, "I'll be ready."

That evening, when we made camp, we hobbled the horses instead of picketing them. We stuffed our bedrolls with branches and made some crude-looking heads out of some sacks we had trade goods in. The whole setup looked rough, but Moses had said that with the poor light and those jaspers seeing what they wanted to, it just might work. Since he'd gone to the mountains some forty-five years ago and still had his hair, I was inclined to believe him. Now we had to wait and see if the renegades would cooperate and hit us tonight.

I do not mind telling you, I was nervous. I had been in my first shooting affair, but that had been in the daylight. This was going to be at night. Pa had been schooling me on this in case it ever happened. You shoot and move off to one side. Shoot and move. Always move after you shoot.

We let our fire burn down, then hid back in the trees a few feet in the shadows, away from our bedrolls. Pa and I loaded the empty chamber on our pistols. Our carbines were with us as well. Moses took out the smoothbore and loaded it with four .36-calibre pistol balls and about ten buckshot pellets.

We waited for what seemed like forever. There were clouds covering the moon, leaving just enough light to make out shadows. The sounds of the night were all around us—frogs croaking, an owl hooting from a nearby tree, and from somewhere out on the prairie, I could hear a coyote howling. All of my senses were on high alert—I was not the least bit tired.

In the middle of the night, the horses started getting restless. One of them nickered nervously and lifted its head, sniffing the air. Then I heard the snap of twigs and saw the flickering of shadows as there was movement on the other side of the burnt-down fire. I don't know how many of them there were; they just stepped out of the brush and started shooting at our bedrolls. Suddenly, one of the attackers screamed; Moses's tomahawk was half buried in his chest. Then, all three of us started firing at the same time. I dropped, pulled my pistol, and fired at where it looked like someone could be. On the far right of our position came a thunderous blast as a sheet of flame shot out toward our attackers.

Time slowed down for me. I remember firing my carbine and emptying my pistol toward the angry blasts of orange flame that were coming our way. Pistol balls were zinging all around me, but I kept firing. In what felt like slow motion, I would shoot to one side of a flash and move. The whole time, there was this loud thundering in my head. After what seemed like an eternity, my pistol was empty. I managed to crawl back to where I had dropped the Warner after my first shot. I had some cartridges in my pocket and reloaded the gun in seconds. Waiting, I saw a flash in the brush, only twenty or so feet off to my left. Taking my time, I waited till I could see the slightest bit of movement. I adjusted the carbine and squeezed the trigger. I rolled to the right, but nothing happened. Someone moaned in the direction I had fired, but I couldn't see anything to get a shot at. Then it was quiet.

I stayed absolutely still for what felt like half an hour, my heart pounding in my head, and then I could hear horses leaving in the distance. A few minutes later, Pa's voice sounded behind me, "I think they pulled out. We will just wait a while. That feller you hit can just keep moaning until Moses is done crawling around, seeing if any of them stayed back playing possum."

We waited, not moving or saying another word. The sun's glow was starting to show on the horizon when Moses gave a whistle from the direction I had last fired my carbine. We got up and started surveying the carnage we had wrought on these would-be assassins. By now, my heart had slowed down, and I was starting to feel a bit weak. Pa said that the excitement from the battle—for that's what it was—was wearing off. He looked at me and asked, "How long do you think the shooting lasted?"

I thought about it. "I don't know. Half an hour or more, I reckon?"

"About five minutes," he answered.

I could see the body of the first renegade that fell, Moses's tomahawk still half buried in his chest. Beside him was another, lying on the ground with a bullet hole through his chest. Off to the left was a third man, who had bled out from a shattered shoulder. Anyone who tells you that a shoulder wound is not serious doesn't know what they're talking about. We continued cautiously toward Moses. As we approached, we could see there was a body on the ground, not far from him. This was the one I'd shot with my Warner. At that range, a 56-50 bullet packs quite a wallop. I had hit him in the meaty area above the belt line.

He looked to be around thirty years of age. Like the others, he was wearing the tattered remains of a uniform, now stained dark with blood. He started moaning again, "For God's sake, help me! I'm hurt bad."

Pa looked down at him with cold eyes. "Where is my daughter? What have you done with her?"

"You mean that yeller-haired gal? The one that Dixon is keeping for his own self?" the derelict piece of humanity whined. "We just wanted to have some fun with her, and she done shot Everett. Well, what were we supposed to do? Then, that feller in the barn stuck Casey with a pitchfork. So we shot him for that."

Moses glared down at the wounded outlaw. "I will say this: you are a hard man to feel bad about shootin', that's for sure. Where is this Dixon headed? To the gold fields or somewhere else?"

"I don't know where," cried the wanna-be killer. "But Mathias, the scout he hired at the big fort, says that depending on the weather, it might be too late to get through the mountain passes. He said something about the Cypress Hills being a good place to winter. And maybe Dixon could even carve out a big piece of land there for himself."

Moses turned to us. "I've heard of the Cypress Hills back when I was in the mountains. Good wintering grounds for some of the tribes. Even some Metis winter there."

Pa looked down at the despicable creature in total disgust. "So, were you just having fun when you murdered those people with the carts, too?"

"No, we needed their provisions, and they didn't want to sell them to us," whimpered the man. "We offered them good money for them supplies 'cuz we really needed them."

"So did they," Pa snapped at him. Then, looking at me, he said grimly, "Jimmy, get a rope and a horse."

Chapter Twelve

The sun was in the sky by the time Pa and I broke camp. We had gathered up the guns of the dead outlaws while we were waiting. They had all been carrying revolvers of various makes. While waiting for Moses to return from scouting, we commenced running a cleaning rod through all the guns.

Then we reloaded all the pistols. Two were Colts in .44-calibre. Pa kept one of these and stuck it in his belt. He handed me another Confederate gun in .36-calibre, saying that I might as well have two pistols in the same calibre. This was a Leech and Rigdon, which was a copy of the Colt Navy. It was to become my favourite, as it was so well-balanced and just pointed naturally to what I wanted to shoot at.

The last pistol was a Remington .44 Army. Pa claimed it was the best-made gun in our whole arsenal.

We were ready to ride out by the time Moses returned from his scouting. Pa handed Moses the Remington and the army holster it came in, saying, "The way things are going around here, you better get used to some newer hardware."

Moses looked over the Remington and grinned. "I reckon you're right there, William." The grin left his face as he looked at me, quietly asking, "How are you feeling, Jimmy? It was a rough night, but we pulled through."

I nodded. "We did, but we still ain't got Judith."

I had never thought of myself as a killer or ever wanted to be a killer. But in all the bloodshed of the past few days, I had seen that with this gang, it was "kill or be killed." I was realizing that we were going to have to be as ruthless as the renegades if we were going to have any hope of getting Judith back safely. I kept remembering the bodies of the people from the burnt-out carts. Especially the poor woman who had been shot in the back so many times.

Moses looked over at Pa. "I think we just might be a whole lot closer to Judith than we figgered. I found where they left their horses. There were sixteen riders when they came, eleven when they left, and two were bleeding. I found another dead one who didn't make it to the horses. His buddies took his hardware with them."

Pa pondered on this. "Do you think they're rattled enough they'd head to their boss? We already know most of them are deserters; it's not like they're the 'bravest of the brave.' Any chance this bunch would figure out this whole shebang just isn't worth it and maybe pull out and head for parts unknown?"

"I doubt it. But we can either trail these guys, or we can keep following the wagon track." Moses looked up at the sky. "Looks like rain coming in. We know Judith is with the wagon. We got no guarantee where those jaspers are gonna go. Whatcha think, William?"

Pa closed his eyes in deep thought, then spoke. "We're most of a couple of days from Qu'Appelle. I'm thinking our best bet is to follow the wagon track and see if it goes to the fort."

We were all in agreement. Wanting to leave last night behind us, we pulled out as soon as we could, with Pa out ahead, riding point.

I noticed that the farther west we rode, the drier it was getting. The grass was shorter, there were fewer and fewer trees, and sometimes we went hours before coming across fresh water. When we came to a small stream in the late afternoon, we stopped and made camp. It was earlier than usual, but we were all getting bone tired—we hadn't slept in over thirty-six hours.

We had no visitors that night. Around midnight, the rain hit again. It had stopped by the time the sun came up but had been heavy enough that it was going to make following any tracks even more difficult. All we could do was keep riding toward Qu'Appelle and hope that's where the wagon was headed. Sometimes, you just gotta gamble and play the odds.

We managed to make the fort with a little daylight to spare. This fort was fairly new; the wood timbers still had a yellow shine to them. It was all wood—no stone walls like there had been back at Fort Garry. It was a Hudson Bay's trading post, quite a bit smaller than Fort Garry, but still had a blacksmith shop and general store, with some living quarters for the staff.

We rode up to the general store, where the trading happened. We all climbed down from our horses, tied them to the hitching rail, and went inside. To avoid any confusion, Pa pulled out his papers right off and told our story.

The trader eyed them and then looked at Pa, saying, "Now it makes sense. A few days ago, there was a wagon and six, maybe seven, riders camped about a half mile west by that grove of trees. Seemed odd. Most folks would've brought the wagon into the fort and filled it with supplies."

Moses spoke up. "They're a sneaky, cowardly lot. Tried to kill us twice since we took up their trail."

I asked, "Did anyone see my sister at any time they were here? She's fairly tall for a girl and has long blonde hair."

"No, we never saw any sign of a girl. I was outside the fort early yesterday morning and noticed they had left." He looked us over. "I take it the killing didn't quite go as they planned?"

"You could put it that way," Moses answered dryly. "There's five of them feeding scavengers a couple days east of here."

"Did they get much for supplies?" Pa asked.

"Mostly staples. You know... flour, sugar, jerky, and some airtights." The trader paused, then added, "Some lead, powder, and caps as well. I can get the receipts if you want."

We looked them over, but there was nothing on the list that was anything special for a girl.

"Any fresh horses around here that we could swap?" Pa asked the trader.

"None in any better shape than yours. We had two real good horses here, but someone took them and left two tired horses and two Yankee double eagles. Didn't think much of it at the time. Seemed a fair swap. Oh, Lord, it was them people you're hunting, wasn't it?" groaned the trader.

"Can't do much about it now," Pa replied. "We'll grab some more supplies quick, then find a place to camp where our horses can graze a bit."

After we made our purchases, we headed out to a nice little spot under some cottonwoods that lined the banks of the Qu'Appelle River.

We hobbled the horses out so they could graze on the lush green grass and then set about making our camp and cooking supper. Once this was done, we called it a day. Moses took first watch, I was on the middle, and Pa did the last one. Thankfully, it turned out to be an uneventful night.

Once it was light enough to see, we broke camp. Pa rode back to the fort, where he took the time to write three letters: one to Governor MacTavish, one to Grandma, and one to his friend Caleb Daniels, the US Army intelligence officer.

Moses and I went over to where the renegades had been camped. After tying our horses a ways back, Moses surveyed the scene and then slowly started walking into the abandoned site. I looked for signs outside the camp, making ever bigger circles. I spotted the tracks where a large group of horses had joined the camp. They would be the fellers that tried to kill us. I then found where all the horses had been watered at the river. It wasn't hard to see where the outfit had pulled out and headed more or less west.

Pa rode up and waited quietly until we had finished looking for signs. I must admit that it did feel good knowing he had confidence in me.

Moses was finished a little ahead of me and then went and stood beside Pa. When I was done, I went over and joined them.

"Well, Jimmy?" Moses asked.

"A group of riders came into camp, maybe at night. The grass wasn't flattened as much as any tracks we've been following. There's a well-trampled place on the riverbank where they watered all the horses a few times. I couldn't see any markers from Judith. I'm hoping that it's just because they were keeping a real tight rein on her this close to the fort."

"Yep, I think they would be doing all they could to hide her." Moses continued, "I'm a thinkin' the girls were took down to the river at night. After they cleaned up, the horses were led to the river and watered, covering up all sign of the girls that way. I figger it had to be our boys from a couple nights ago who rode into the camp. Jimmy's right. It was at night. Then the whole crew pulled out before morning."

Then his voice became solemn. "But William... I found some soft dirt where the horses had trampled the ground real good. I think they might have buried someone. We gotta check it out."

Pa looked up. I could see the worry coming over his face before he quietly spoke. "Let's hope it's not our girl."

My stomach churned with dread as I went and grabbed the shovel we kept from the burnt-out carts. I carefully started digging. We all breathed with relief as I unearthed the body of a man.

Pal let out a ragged breath. "Thank God it's not Judith."

The man was clad in the remains of a faded blue uniform. As we brushed off the rest of the dirt, we could see that he had been hit by a pistol ball and some buckshot.

"Guess we did better than we thought," uttered Moses. "In the camp, I saw at least three places where wounded men had been tended to. I would assume this jasper was one of them."

We refilled the shallow grave and walked over to our horses.

Pa began talking. "Here's the way I see it. This Dixon has ideas of carving out a little kingdom for himself. The war's over in the States, and there are all kinds of riffraff wandering around. He hears about what's happening up here and realizes there might be an opportunity for a fellow with a small army to claim a chunk of Rupert's Land for himself. This man is used to power and taking what he wants. He probably comes from wealth and has lost it through the war. He's possibly a former slave owner. He sees Judith while his men are raiding the farm, and he wants her. So he takes her. He doesn't worry about any consequences. Judith and Ollie are just poor farm folk to him."

Pa continued, "He gets up here to this country and hears of the gold rush out in the western mountains. Remember, for the last four years, a gold rush up here wasn't the big news back home.

"By now, he realizes he is being followed. We've killed eight of his men, so he has a problem. He also knows that a pile of gold makes it a whole lot easier to carve out an empire, or, at the very least, be a big wheel up here."

Moses spoke up next. "So what does he do now? He knows we're still after him. His hold on these men will be getting less and less. Most have already deserted one army when the goin' got rough. It's gettin' too late in the year to head for the gold fields. If I was him and had a purdy girl, I wouldn't want to winter anywhere with the remnants of this crowd. How does he get shut of them, though? He has promised them gold or money, and they ain't seen any of that. At the very least, his men are thinkin' about a new leader. And where does this scout he hired, Mathias, fit in?"

"Pa, none of this is good for Judith. As bad as things are, it would be even worse if this Dixon loses control. Even though we think he might've headed out on his own with Judith, we can't be sure, can we?" I asked.

"No, we can't," both Pa and Moses answered. "We have to keep following the wagon tracks."

We mounted up and set out, with Moses in front scouting. I found my mind wandering back to all the times that Judith and I had gone out riding together, especially after our mother had died. The two of us had been inseparable. We would put a bridle on Pa's old saddle mare, Quincy, and ride her bareback. Grandma always reminded us not to ride any farther than the trees past the end of the oat field. When we got older, we each had our own horse. We had spent hours riding together, exploring the countryside.

The wagon tracks were still quite clear and easy to follow. Eating jerky on the go and stopping only long enough to switch horses, we were pretty sure we had gained on our quarry. We rode hard for two and a half days, stopping less, eating on the go, riding till dark, and making a quick camp.

It was late in the afternoon. I was on point, riding up to a slight slope on the edge of some brush in a bit of a hollow. The top of the rise was devoid of any cover. Anyone riding over that would be skylined to whoever was on the other side. Even this crowd could set up a good shooting gallery here, and we would be the targets.

I left my horse in the little hollow. In my saddle bags were a pair of moccasins that I had bought back in Fort Garry. I swapped out my boots for the moccasins and commenced to crawl through the brush to get as close to the peak of the rise as I could. Pa and Moses would see my horse and boots and would stay back unless trouble showed up.

As I inched my way through, I realized that slightly to my left, the brush ran right to the crest of the hill. Now, I'm not talking trees, but buckbrush, maybe a foot and a half high at best. Moses had taught me well, and I knew I could make it up through that to the peak without being seen. It took twenty minutes or so, and when I parted the brush at the top to look down the other side, I could see their camp!

Relief raced through my body. We'd done it—we'd caught up to them! The camp was about 300 yards away. They had stopped for the day. Maybe a little early, but it was too good a spot to pass up if someone was on your trail.

There was a small stream—just a trickle—but enough for a camp and to water the horses. The wagon was parked about thirty feet from the stream. The horses were grazing on picket ropes. To the left of the wagon and to the right were some tarp shelters.

I took my time, carefully scanning and looking for Judith. My heart sank when I didn't see any sign of her golden hair. If she was here, she *had* to be in the wagon.

I had counted fourteen men moving around, some doing camp chores such as gathering wood for the fire while others were cleaning their guns. I hadn't seen any guards. It looked to me that a rough-looking fella wearing a green shirt and a grey kepi was giving the orders.

I quietly worked my way through the brush back down to my horse. I mounted up and rode back to where Pa and Moses were waiting.

"We caught up!" I whispered excitedly, as if, on the other side of the hill, over half a mile away, they could hear me.

"Any sign of Judith?" Pa immediately asked.

"I didn't see her. But she could be in the wagon." I then scraped the grass off a patch of ground, and using twigs and little stones, I drew a rough layout of the camp.

"Well, boys," Moses said low and slow, "I'll go out left and find any guards that way." Looking at Pa, he said, "William, what do you think of going right, taking out any guards, and then covering the men in the tarps? If things go right, they'll sleep through it all."

He switched his gaze to me. "Jimmy, you will have to walk a few hundred yards out to the north and at least four hundred yards west, then come back south so that you'll come out behind the wagon. If you don't hear anything, sneak up careful and get a look in that wagon. If the girls are in there, you get them out. Go straight west out from the wagon and keep moving. If all goes as planned, me and William will catch up to you on the horses we grab. If it doesn't go as planned, get back to our horses and get the girls to safety. Either we'll be dead, or we'll join up with you. Do *not* come back for us! Get Judith!"

I nodded with grim resolve as Moses's words sunk in. This is what we had come to do. There was no time to be scared. It was up to me to get Judith out of that wagon.

We waited until it was dark. There was a bit of moonlight, which was obscured by light cloud cover.

I set out, walking with Pa for the first couple hundred yards. Then he tapped me on the shoulder, and we split up. I kept walking and counting my steps. When I had counted 250 steps, I turned left and continued walking and counting. At 400, I turned left again and made another 450 steps. Through an opening in the trees, I could see the glowing embers where the fire had been.

I waited, counting to 300, which I figured would give Pa and Moses a little more time to take out the guards. I moved carefully toward the wagon, taking advantage of any brush or trees, such as they were. It took what felt like an eternity, but I finally made it. I stopped, listening carefully. Not hearing anybody walking around the wagon, I climbed up, slowly inching aside the canvas. I sensed sudden movement inside the wagon, and before I could react, I felt the sharp edge of cold steel held tight against my throat.

"Move an inch, and I will cut you," hissed a female voice with a slight French accent.

"Wait, I'm Judith's brother! I'm here to rescue you two," I whispered as forcefully as I could while feeling the edge on my throat.

At that moment, the moon came out from behind the cloud, just long enough for the girl to see my face.

The jackknife was gone from my throat in an instant. I poked my head farther into the wagon. She was alone! "Where's Judith?" I frantically choked out.

"The leader took her away in the night before we left the fort," the girl sadly whispered.

I was stunned and felt like I'd been kicked in the stomach, but quickly snapped back to my senses when the girl urgently tugged on my sleeve. "We have to get out of here. Now!"

We wasted no time in climbing down out of the wagon. We were quietly moving away from its side when someone fired a couple of rounds with a pistol. This was followed by a few more shots, and then all hell broke loose.

We started running as fast as we could straight away from the wagon until we had to slow down to catch our breath.

"How on earth do you have a knife?" I gasped.

"They took my hunting knife when they captured me. But never found the little jackknife I had hidden away."

I figured we were a good 500 yards from camp when we could hear some horses coming up behind us. I heard the low cooing of a dove, and I cooed back. Soon Moses rode up bareback and leading two horses.

"Two's all I could get without raising much ruckus. I slipped the halters on some of the others and cut the rest loose. Them boys is on foot now." Then he noticed that the girl with me wasn't Judith. He looked behind her, and his eyes widened in shock. "Where in the hell's Judith? What happened?"

"Dixon lit out with her days ago back at Fort Qu'Appelle," I answered as I took the shank from him and swung aboard one of the horses. I noticed that the girl I rescued wasted no time getting mounted either.

"Where's Pa?" I half yelled to be heard above the horses.

"He's a comin'," the old man hollered back.

We made a big circle to the north and came around back to where we had left our horses. They were still there, saddled and ready.

By now, all the shooting had stopped. Over at the renegade camp, it was absolute pandemonium. There was yelling and cussing, the likes of which I had never heard!

I was starting to get worried. Where was Pa? Moses figured he would've just dropped to the ground and crawled away once the shooting stopped.

"What if one of those pistol balls those jaspers was a'shootin' hit him?" I spoke low.

"We'll give him five more minutes, then I'll go looking." I could hear the worry in Moses's voice.

I started counting. At 433, Pa staggered over the little rise in front of us and collapsed at my feet.

Chapter Thirteen

I bent down and started to look him over. Moses was beside me in a flash. I ran my hand under Pa's shirt and felt blood. It was leaking out from a small hole just under his right shoulder. Feeling behind the shoulder, I found the small bump of a pistol ball under the skin. I breathed a sigh of relief. A large rifle bullet, if it had hit bone, would have shattered the whole shoulder.

"All we can do right now is plug that leak tight. And then we gotta get outta here," Moses whispered.

The girl I'd rescued had been rummaging through our packs. By the time I got up to grab bandages and alcohol, she was already kneeling on the ground beside Pa. She splashed a little of the alcohol on the wound and slapped one of Grandma's bandage rags on it, then commenced to wrap a piece of cloth around Pa's chest and tie it tight.

Looking up to Moses and me, she whispered, "We have to take that bullet out as soon as we can. But I know we have to leave now."

We got Pa up on a horse, and I went to climb up behind to hold him on. She shook her head at me, saying,

"No, I'll ride with him. I'm lighter. It'll be easier on the horse."

Moses and I held Pa in place while she swung herself up behind him. We mounted quickly and, leading all the extra horses, we headed east back toward Fort Qu'Appelle.

I looked over at the girl holding Pa. Her long black hair hung loose, reaching halfway down her back. She was smaller than Judith yet seemed to have no trouble supporting Pa in place. I rode up beside her, saying, "By the way, I'm Jimmy Munro. That's my pa, William Munro. And that's my grandfather, Moses Munro, riding guard behind us."

"I am Celine Fournier. Thank you for saving me."

We kept walking the horses as fast as we dared. We didn't do much talking, as we were listening intently for any signs that we were being followed. We had ridden about two hours when Pa started to moan.

We stopped on the edge of a small poplar grove. Celine had Pa half lowered off the horse before Moses and I could even get to her side to help. What a girl to have around in a tight spot!

"I'll cut the bullet out. I did all the patching up in our family for years. My mother had arthritis in her hands, so that left me." She looked at me. "I'll need a fire as quick as you can get it going." She moved her gaze to Moses. "Can you roll him over so I can wash off where I must cut?"

"Yes, ma'am," Moses replied, almost in shock at this girl having a handle on the situation so quickly.

We were on the east side of the trees, so my fire wouldn't show to the west. But even so, I kept it small. I then helped Moses move Pa over to the edge of the fire.

The girl had been rubbing alcohol over the bump and rubbed on a little more after we moved him to where she could see.

"Knife." She reached her hand out to me. I handed her my knife, and she poured some of the alcohol on it. She then commenced to rub the blade with a cloth until it shone almost like a mirror. Holding the blade of my knife in the flames of the fire for a few seconds, she then looked at us and said, "Ready?"

We held Pa down firmly so he couldn't move while she cut the skin. Thankfully all she had to do was put the tip of the blade under the ball, and it popped out through the slit she had made. Grabbing a needle and thread out of the pack, she dipped them in the alcohol, also splashing some over her fingers in the process. Three stitches were all it took to close the wound. She had found some salve in the pack as well, so after pouring more alcohol on the stitches, she applied some salve over the wound and put a bandage over the whole area.

"Roll him over. I've got to fix up the front."

We gently rolled Pa over. While I held the bandage on the back of his shoulder in place, she wiped away the blood on his front. We could see the entry hole made by the ball. At least it was only a .36-calibre and not bigger. The bleeding had almost stopped and needed only two stitches to close. She then rinsed the area with alcohol, rubbed on more of the salve, and bandaged it. Wrapping a long rag around him, she did it in such a way that it held both bandages—front and back—in place. She worked quickly and efficiently, with the whole process taking less than twenty minutes.

While she was stowing the medical supplies back into the pack, Moses and I fashioned a travois, which we hooked to one of the pack horses. Putting the pack on the travois with Pa, we got moving, with the girl in the lead. Moses and I brought up the rear in case those boys behind us had caught some horses and were after us.

By late morning, we had to stop. The horses had been ridden hard and needed a rest. We had to rest as well, not having slept at all last night.

We settled Pa as comfortably as we could on some bed rolls on the ground. Moses looked over to Celine, saying, "That was a mighty fine job of doctoring, ma'am. Thank you."

"Merci, I did what I could." Looking earnestly at us, she said, "Thank you for getting me away from those terrible men." Her eyes filled with tears, and her voice choked as she said, "They murdered my entire family—even my mother. The only reason they didn't harm me is their leader wanted to sell me in Fort Benton to a bad man. I am in your debt."

I stared at her, my mind racing. "They were going to sell you in Fort Benton?! Is that what Dixon is going to do with Judith, too?"

Celine shook her head. "No, I'm pretty sure he wants her for himself."

Moses then solemnly spoke. "We found your folks, ma'am. We buried them as best we could, and William spoke a few words over them. When we got to Fort Ellice, we let them know what had happened. The Bay men were going to bring them back to the fort for a proper Christian burial."

Celine's dark-brown eyes looked up at Moses. "Merci, monsieur."

Regaining her composure, she gazed down at Pa, murmuring, "I hope he comes around soon. He lost a lot of blood. We will have to wait here a bit so he can rest."

"You'd best get some rest too, ma'am," I said as I was getting my Warner out of its scabbard. "You too, Moses. I'll take first watch."

I kept watch for a couple of hours, constantly checking in all four directions. The more I thought about it, the more I reckoned we had a fifty-fifty chance. This rabble wasn't as well led as they had been, and they were already down by at least fifteen men, not counting the wounded. Any damage that had been done when Pa opened up on them must have rattled some of them. If we were lucky, some might decide this was just not worth it and leave.

Moses came to relieve me. We stood together quietly, looking to the west, and spotted five riders coming over a small rise toward us. With Pa on a travois, we knew we didn't have the slightest chance of outrunning them.

"We'll have to fight the bastards again," growled Moses. "At least the odds are getting whittled down. Jimmy, you figger you could hit anything with that Reb sniper gun your Pa kept? I know he took that side-mounted scope off it and packed it away, but the sights that are still on it go up to twelve hundred yards."

"I reckon I could hit a man on a horse that was standing still at five, maybe even six hundred yards," I answered.

"Go grab the gun, Jimmy. These bastards don't realize we have it. I'll keep watching them."

I went and got the Whitworth from our packs. While I was loading, Celine was checking on Pa.

She looked over to me. "Give me a gun, and I'll stay by your father."

I glanced around the camp and spied Moses's sawed-off musket. Making sure it was capped and loaded, I handed it to her. "Anyone that ain't me or Moses, you just point this at them and squeeze the trigger."

Joining Moses again, I could see our pursuers were getting closer. Moses murmured, "Just crossed the half-mile line." Looking through Pa's army field glasses that I had brought back with me, I recognized some of the men I had seen in the camp yesterday afternoon. "It's them all right," I muttered. "I recognize that feller in the green shirt and the grey kepi. He was the one giving orders yesterday."

"Let's hope they stop on that rise when they get to it. They're gonna need a little time to figure out what to do about us. Must want that girl pretty bad, though," Moses surmised.

"She's probably worth a fair bit in Fort Benton," I commented. "She is mighty easy on the eyes when you see her in the daylight."

Moses looked at me and grinned. "I figured you'd get around to noticing that sooner or later."

About then, the riders stopped. As Moses predicted, they seemed to be trying to come up with a plan.

I was lying in the grass with the rifle resting on a log, the sights raised to 600 yards. I had a clear shot at the leader and was just about to chance it when I heard Moses snap, "Hold it! They're sending a feller up under a white flag. They don't know how that worked out for the last bunch who tried it. They're stalling for time. Either got more coming or some working their way behind us. We gotta drop these guys quick!"

At 300 yards, the rider stopped and shouted, "We just want the girl. Hand her over, and we'll let you go. We know one of you is wounded. If you don't give her to us now, we'll come back again after our friends catch their horses, and you'll be killed off once and for all."

My front sight covered most of my target above his horse's head.

Click. Moses pulled the hammer back on his old mountain rifle. "You ready? On three."

I took in a deep breath and started to let it out slowly.

"One… two… three."

We squeezed the triggers, and both rifles roared to life. We heard the thump of Moses's ball hitting Mr. White Flag. Moses had squeezed his trigger a tiny fraction of a second behind me on purpose, so there wasn't much difference on the time our bullets hit. The feller who appeared to be the leader flinched in his saddle and then fell off his horse.

The three remaining riders, apparently deciding they had better places to be, spun their horses around and lit out of there like greased lightning.

A loud BOOM echoed through the little grove of trees. We each pulled a pistol and ran like hell through the trees back to Celine and Pa.

Twenty-five yards away, two men were writhing and moaning in pain. One, with black hair and dark stubble, was shot in the chest, his faded blue shirt covered in blood.

He coughed up some blood, then his head sank to one side and fell limp as he died. The other one, who looked to be in his early thirties, was lying on the ground, clutching at his left thigh. He tried to grab his pistol when he saw us approaching. I was over him in a flash, pointing my revolver in his face. "Wanna think that idea over?"

"Well, feller," Moses said as he walked over to us and looked down. "Appears to me you are having a bad day. Looks like you went and got yourself a pistol ball and a little buckshot in your sorry carcass."

"How many of you useless scum are left?" I demanded.

He got all sullen-looking and stayed silent.

"Jimmy, you remember me telling you about the trapper I found after some Rees had burnt his feet?" Moses grinned at me and winked. "You start a fire. I'll take his boots off. Maybe I can scalp him alive for good measure."

That did the trick; the wounded man started to wail. "Wait, wait! I'll talk. There are fourteen left. Only seven of us could catch our horses. Four of them back at camp are hurt bad. If you'll just let me go, I swear I'll go home to Tennessee and never come back."

"Where is Dixon going with my sister?" I growled at him.

"I don't know," whined the sorry lowlife. "Dixon promised us we'd all get rich and have a pile of land. But then him and the scout pulled out with that blonde girl while we was camped at the fort. We got up in the morning, and they was gone. Wilson was furious!"

"Is Wilson the one calling the shots? Green shirt, grey kepi?" I questioned.

"Yeah. He plans on killin' you and getting back that girl you took from us so he can sell her to a brothel owner in Fort Benton."

"Guess he had a bad day, too," Moses drawled. "He fell off his horse about six hundred yards out yonder. The three still mounted lit out of here like they don't plan on seein' these parts again."

I heard footsteps come up behind me. It was Celine with Pa's Warner carbine in her hands. She glared down at the man with total hatred and disgust. "I saw you shoot my maman!" she spat at him. She swung the muzzle of the carbine and her finger squeezed down on the trigger. In a split second, the space between his eyes erupted in blood and bone.

She dropped the gun and fell to the ground, sobbing.

Moses looked at me and nodded toward her. "You stay with her, and I'll go check on your Pa."

Kneeling down on the ground beside her, I awkwardly put my arm around her while she cried quietly for a few minutes on my shoulder. I broke the silence. "Ma'am, I'm sorry. I know you've been through hell. But we have to get moving again in case any of those jaspers build up enough courage to come back."

"Please, call me Celine."

"Okay, ma'am... er, Celine," I stammered. "We better go check on Pa."

We walked back to the fire. Pa was awake, pale but looking alert. Moses had been giving him some water from what we had boiled earlier. It was cool by now, and Pa was thirsty.

Celine dug out some jerky and some hardtack for him to chew on. Then we built up the fire enough for her to fry up some dough that she made with flour, sugar, water, and some bacon grease we'd kept. She told us this wasn't the way her maman had made bannock, but she used what we had. Pa needed energy and something to get him perked up a bit.

While she was feeding Pa, Moses and I gathered the hardware from the four attackers we'd sent for judgment.

The so-called leader of this bunch had a Navy Colt and a muzzle-loading carbine. The one Moses dropped just had the Enfield rifle with the white flag still tied to it.

Celine's two attackers had a Colt pistol and another Enfield between them. While the ones out front had been distracting us, they had snuck up on our camp through a dry water run. We were lucky enough to find their two horses, still tied up where they had left them, and led them back to our camp. Now the travois horse wouldn't have to pull the weight of the packs as well as Pa.

When we returned to the fire, Moses looked to Pa, saying, "We have to keep moving, William, in case some of those outlaws build up enough courage to try us again. I don't think they will—they haven't done very well so far, and now they got no leader—but we can't take that chance. And we have to get back to the fort so we can catch up to our girl."

Pa nodded. "Just help me on the travois. I'll be okay." Looking up at Celine, he said, "I've got a good doctor here."

We saddled up and headed east toward Qu'Appelle. It would be a lot slower going, dragging the travois, and we knew it meant that Dixon would be gaining even more ground on us. But with Pa hurt, there wasn't anything else we could do. We had to put our frustration aside and just keep going as best as we could. We figured we could still make it to the fort in a little under four days.

Chapter Fourteen

For two days, we made reasonable time travelling on the cart trail back to the fort. Even though we were trying to make up some time, a horse and travois could only travel so fast, especially with a wounded man on it.

Now that the pistol ball was out of Pa and the leaks were plugged, there was still all the damage caused by the bullet on its way through. Luckily, the path of the ball went just under any bone as it entered the front and had come out on an angle, just missing the shoulder blade. However, it had torn through a lot of different muscles. Pa was in considerable pain any time he tried to move.

We had stopped for an afternoon break when Celine took Moses and me aside. Speaking low, she whispered, "He is getting a fever. I cleaned the wound as good as I could, but there is always a chance of infection. If we get close to any red willow, I will need bark to make tea. This will help keep the fever down."

I swallowed hard. I knew this was serious. "I'll go have a look around for some willow. There should be some around a pothole or little slough, even if it's dry."

I saddled up a fresh horse and rode ahead on the trail for a ways. I only had to ride for about twenty minutes until I spotted a dry hollow full of willows. I was getting down off my horse when I caught a whiff of decaying meat. My horse was getting almighty skittish, too. I pulled out my Warner. Then I heard a crashing through the bushes, followed by a low grunt and a growl. I tried to hold the horse, but he reared up, yanked the lines right out of my hand, and took off on the run.

I was pretty sure there was a bear nearby. And being this far out on the prairies, I strongly suspected it wasn't one of the little black bears like we had at home. I'd heard enough stories about grizzly bears from Moses while growing up to know I was in trouble. In my pocket were some cartridges for my carbine. I dug out two of them and placed them between the fingers of my left hand. Then I started backing away, not wanting a fight but wanting to be as ready as I could. The 56-50 was not a big cartridge, and no one would make it first pick for tackling a grizzly bear, but it was what I had with me.

I could hear the bear huffing as he lumbered toward me. When it came out of the willows, I could see the silver-tipped brown fur and the big hump on its shoulders. Then it reared up on its hind feet, roaring. Good Lord, it stood ten feet tall and had claws four inches long! This had to be a grizzly. And I was starting to get the impression that he was not too happy about being disturbed.

I was steadily backing up the whole time the bear stood growling at me. Putting my carbine in the crook of my arm, I took out my pistol and fired it twice in the air.

The griz lowered back onto all fours, then shook his head, his eyes never leaving me. I kept retreating and fired my pistol a couple more times. By now, I was getting close to eighty yards away from the bear. I kept backing up.

The bear finally gave a grunt and then turned back to his business in the trees.

I shakily holstered my pistol and kept retreating backward for another few minutes until Moses rode up, leading a horse.

Looking down at me and then at the willows in the distance, he heaved a sigh of relief. "Bear in them willows?"

"Yep, a big griz. And he can have them! We'll find Celine some more in another spot."

We rode for a bit until we found another patch of willows, minus a bear. While we were riding, Moses had looked over at me. "Jim, you showed some mighty good judgment there just now. That was the first thing I learned when I went to the mountains—never get in a fight with a griz if you can avoid it. I saw what Hugh Glass looked like after a griz mauled him. He survived but came as close to going under as anyone I ever knew."

Celine smiled warmly at me as I handed her the willows. I had to admit, that girl sure had a pretty smile. I watched her as she started brewing the tea for Pa until I noticed Moses watching me watch her.

My horse had made his way back to camp before Moses and I had returned. Once he was unsaddled, I got my pistol out and commenced to clean and reload it. That reminded me about Pa's Colts. I dug them out of the packs and cleaned and reloaded them as well.

I then thought of the hardware we had taken from the last bunch to attack us. I found the Navy Colt and cleaned it, then loaded and capped it. I put the pistol in the saddlebags on the saddle Celine rode.

It was while I was doing up the flap on the saddlebag that it hit me: Moses had called me "Jim"! Til now, I had always been "Jimmy." I realized he didn't see me as a boy anymore. I sure hoped I could live up to it.

Once Pa was fed a little more jerky and a bowl of willow bark tea, we mounted up and continued on our way.

Celine's tea helped bring Pa's fever down, but he was still warm. And by the next day, his fever was starting to climb again. There weren't any telltale red streaks of infection yet, but if we couldn't get that fever down, Pa could still die. We knew we needed to find a pond, or preferably a stream, to lay him in. And soon.

Moses was scouting ahead in the afternoon when he came riding back into camp earlier than expected. "Found a cool spring about two miles from here off to the north a bit." He continued, "There's some tipis there already, and I don't know any of the tribes out here."

"I can talk to them if they are Cree, Assiniboine, or Saulteaux." Celine added, "My family traded with all three tribes. My grand-mere was Saulteaux."

"Well, we better go get acquainted. William needs to be cooled down." Moses took the lead rope from Celine and headed toward the spring and the Indian camp.

We were halfway there when we were met by four warriors dressed in breechcloths and deerskin leggings. Celine rode ahead, and we could see her talking back and forth with who we assumed to be the chief of this camp.

After what seemed to be a long conversation, she turned to us, saying, "They are Assiniboine on their way back to the Cypress Hills from trading at the fort." She continued, "They have heard of the White Hair and his hunt for his granddaughter. We are welcome to stay by their camp and put our wounded warrior in the cool water."

Moses nodded to the leader. "Tell him we are much obliged."

The Indian nodded back in return, and we all rode to the camp. It wasn't a large camp—six lodges, each about fifteen feet in diameter, set up in a circle with an opening on the east side toward the sun. The encampment was set up on the east side of the spring.

Moses told me this was pretty much a common setup for most of the Plains tribes' summer camps. Usually, the camp was on the east side of the water, in case of a prairie fire, the prevailing wind being from the west.

There looked to be at least thirty people in the camp. The men were tending to the horses as the women prepared supper. There were some little kids running and giggling as they chased each other past some elders who were braiding leather halters. All stopped and watched with interest as we rode past them to the spring, then returned to their duties.

We lowered Pa from the travois and laid him gently in the water. While not cold, the water was quite cool, and we hoped it would do the trick. If the fever wouldn't come down, Pa was in real trouble. While Celine stayed with Pa, Moses and I set up camp.

One of the men from the Indian camp came over to us. He was a tall man with greying hair in braids who carried himself with confidence. He stood quietly while we were picketing the horses. Once we had finished our task, he started to speak. "White Hair, my wife is a medicine woman. She can help your wounded warrior. The girl tells us he is your son."

Moses, who had developed a great respect for Native medicine while wintering with the Crow and the Shoshone during his trapping years, nodded his head. "I would appreciate that very much."

The man went back to fetch his wife, and soon some of the women went to the spring and carried Pa back to a tipi.

We went over to see how Pa was coming along. He was shivering when we got there. The medicine woman had wrapped him up and set him by the warm fire. She had prepared a bowl of herbs and plants mixed in a broth made from bone marrow. She spooned it all into Pa, and not long after she finished feeding him, he fell into a deep sleep.

The medicine woman looked up at us and started speaking in Assiniboine. Celine translated, "He will sleep until tomorrow. We will see how he is then."

"Can you tell her thank you from all of us?" I asked Celine.

The medicine woman's husband was waiting outside the tent. "I am the only one here who speaks much of the white man's tongue. I am called Tall Bull. At the trading fort, I was told about your search for your granddaughter, a yellow-haired girl. Eight nights ago, we were camped north of the fort. We heard a small group of horses going north up the trail toward Fort Carlton. Maybe knowing this will help you in your search."

Moses then commenced to tell Tall Bull about our journey and our recent fights with the bunch we had rescued Celine from.

Tall Bull gravely nodded. "We will keep a lookout for any of these bad men and try to avoid them. I will talk to the chief, but we are only eight warriors and have our families to protect."

Moses looked over at me, and I could tell we were thinking along the same lines. "I think we can help you with that. How are you fixed for guns?" he asked.

"We have three trade guns from the Bay men and an old gun of my grandfather's from back when he traded with the Frenchmen," Tall Bull answered.

Moses grinned. "Come with us," he said and gestured for Tall Bull to follow.

We walked back to our camp and dug out the two Enfield rifles. Seeing as we had also taken the ammunition when we gathered up the guns from the previous owners, we could give these people the rifles and close to seventy cartridges and a tin of a hundred caps.

"We don't need all these," Moses told Tall Bull. "Use them to protect your families."

Tall Bull was left almost speechless. He managed to say, "Thank you, White Hair and Jim. You are most generous. We will remember you." He carried the guns back to their camp.

When Celine got back to camp from talking with the women, she was carrying a big pot of soup that the chief's wife had sent with her. We dug right in. I had no idea what all was in it, but I do not mind saying, after the last few days of jerky and hardtack, it tasted almighty good.

I accompanied Celine when she returned the cooking pot to the chief's wife. The chief came over to us and started talking to Celine. He was a large man with a barrel chest who had an eagle feather woven into his hair. He was even taller than Pa, and Pa stood six foot one in his sock feet.

When he had finished speaking, Celine turned to me and translated, "He thanks you for the rifles. He also said we could sleep well tonight. He has people on watch."

"Tell him we are grateful," I replied.

Celine relayed my message, and the chief nodded at me. He then returned to speak with his men.

Walking back to our own camp with Celine seemed to me about the most peaceful and natural thing in the world. With her shining dark hair and deep brown eyes, she was one of the prettiest girls I had ever seen. And I had never met a girl who was so easy to be around. For those few minutes, we could almost forget the horrors and the dangers we had already faced or the ones yet to come.

When we got there, Moses was already asleep. We turned in for the night, and for the first time in weeks, we all got a full night's sleep.

All of us were already awake as the sun was just starting to peek over the horizon. The first thing we did was head over to the Assiniboine camp to see if there was any improvement in Pa.

We weren't even all the way to Tall Bull's tent before Pa walked out to meet us. I couldn't believe my eyes! I heaved a huge sigh of relief. It looked like Pa was going to make it!

Now, I ain't saying he was a bundle of energy, but he was on his feet and making his way toward us. Tall Bull was walking beside him. Pa's arm was in a sling and held tight against his body, but he looked at us and asked how soon we'd be ready to ride.

Moses skeptically looked at Pa. "You sure made a quick recovery. But, William, are you sure you can manage a horse? We could still pull you on the travois for a day or two."

"I can ride," Pa grimly answered, settling the question right then and there.

Moses went to our pack of trade goods and returned with a new trade knife, a hatchet, some flints, and a Hudson Bay blanket. Handing the knife and blanket to Celine, he asked, "Would you take these and give them to the medicine woman as a thank you from us?"

He then turned to Tall Bull and handed him the flints and the hatchet. "Won't hurt to have some extra flints for your trade guns."

We then said our goodbyes and started saddling up.

Moses, Celine, and I were all leading pack animals and the extra horses we had acquired. Pa was riding an Appaloosa, the smoothest horse we had in the bunch. Even so, he had to have been hurting a lot, but he never said a word.

At midday, we stopped to eat. Moses and I helped Pa off his horse and made him rest under a tree while we got a fire going for Celine to fix up some dinner.

Pa actually fell asleep while the bacon was cooking, so we let him sleep for a bit before we woke him to eat.

Once we finished eating, Moses and I saddled up some fresh horses, and we hit the trail again.

Even with the extra stops to let Pa rest, we still managed to make pretty good time. And late afternoon, two days later, we rode through the gates of Fort Qu'Appelle.

Chapter Fifteen

We tied our horses in front of the trading store alongside a Red River cart and went inside. The trader was busy settling up with a Metis feller. Once their business was done, Moses and Celine struck up a conversation with the cart owner. Pa and I started talking to the trader.

We recounted what had happened since we'd last seen him. He looked at us almost in a state of disbelief. "You mean, you three pretty much took out most of the killers of Celine's family?"

"Maybe not all," I replied, "But most of them. And some of the ones who are left are wounded, and they haven't got many horses. There's a small group of Assiniboine that will more than likely end up with the rest of the horses. That riffraff won't be causing much trouble for the immediate future."

I then asked if Pa could sleep with a roof over his head for a couple of days. Now, admittedly, this was the first Pa had heard of this, and he wasn't gonna have anything to do with this idea. But Moses had overheard me and came over to join us, leaving Celine with the Metis man.

Looking back, we maybe should have told Pa our plan. But knowing Pa, we figured it would be a pretty hard sell. On the trail, Moses, Celine, and I could only see one way that had a snowball's chance in hell of getting Judith back. And it meant we would have to leave Pa somewhere for a few days to heal.

We had come to the conclusion that, as crazy as it sounded, Dixon was going to try to make the gold fields in Barkerville before winter. We couldn't think of any other reason why he would be headed north up the Carlton Trail. What he'd done to convince his scout, Mathias, to even try this late in the year was beyond anything we could figure.

Celine's family had been traders with various tribes all the way to the Rockies, and she'd put her foot down pretty hard when Moses and I had started to come up with a plan.

"I know a shorter way to the Yellowhead Pass. And if you two think you're leaving me behind, you've got another thing coming! Judith kept me from giving up after I watched my family murdered. She was always sure that you would come for her, and she told me how she had been leaving messages when she could. She told me to hang on and that help was on its way. She was all that gave me hope in those days after I was taken, and I am damn sure going to help rescue her," she had declared in her French accent, with her dark eyes flashing.

Moses looked at me, "You wanna tell her to stay?"

"No, sir, I ain't gonna get her any more riled up," I replied.

"Me neither," he mumbled. "And besides, she's right. We don't know a faster way to the Yellowhead."

The hard part was gonna be convincing Pa that he wasn't up to riding forty or more miles a day for what could be three weeks or longer.

To get Pa to go along with our plan, we let Moses do the talking. "William," he said slowly and deliberately, "You are one of the toughest men I know. But, with that shoulder, you know you would be slowing us down. You could ride at a little slower pace up the Carlton Trail. And you've got the power to deputize someone to travel with you in case you catch up to Dixon before we cut them off."

"That cart driver I was talking to—Leonard Trottier—happens to be kin of Celine's, and he figures he could travel with you. He had a good trading season and was gonna go on the fall buffalo hunt, but he figures there are lots of hunters, so he's willing to be sworn in as a constable." Looking Pa in the eye, Moses continued, "You know you won't be able to ride as hard as we'll need to if we're gonna have any chance of getting Judith back. I know this plan has a chance of failing, but it's all we got."

Pa looked back at Moses, then slowly nodded. "I know, and you're right. Better let me meet my new deputy. And then we'll see about getting cleaned up, and find us some new clothes. What's left of these ones pretty much stand up on their own."

When we rode through the gates of the fort at sunup the next morning, we were wearing new linen pants and shirts, including Celine. We left Pa behind with his new deputy. Moses had told Leonard to keep Pa at the fort for at least four days before heading up the trail. I wasn't too sure how well that would work, but as Moses said, it was worth a try.

I had to admit, I had a hollow feeling in the pit of my stomach, leaving without Pa. After these past few weeks on the trail, I could sure see why that old general had relied on Pa so much. I realized that now Moses was going to be counting more and more on me. I had some mighty big boots to fill.

Moses, Celine, and I headed west, each of us leading a spare horse. We rode for two days to skirt the south side of Last Mountain Lake. We were travelling light and fast, taking only food we could cram into our saddle bags. Once past the lake, we started to angle toward the northwest.

Our first big obstacle would be crossing the South Saskatchewan River. Celine knew of a place we should be able to get our horses across this late in the year.

I noticed the water holes were getting farther apart, and the grass was getting a little drier looking.

That night in camp, I asked Celine if it was going to keep getting drier the farther west we went.

She thought for a minute before answering my question. "It will stay like it is here until we reach the river. It is drier farther west, but we will be travelling on the north edge of the dry country." She paused a few seconds. "Once across the river, water does get more scarce, but not as dry as it gets farther south of where we'll be travelling. We will have a dry camp or two but should come across water every day. I know of some small lakes. About four days after we cross the river, we get to the swift-running creek that flows into a big lake. It's early September, so it will be mostly dry, but there will be potholes, and the hills on the southeast of the creek valley have lots of springs that run year-round."

Moses spoke up. "Sounds a whole lot better than a couple of deserts I crossed back when I was trapping."

Conversation kinda dried up after that, as we were all getting tired. As I drifted off to sleep, I thought about how Celine had more than carried her weight since joining us. Any thoughts I initially had of her slowing us down were long gone. Now, it was hard to imagine her not being with us.

After three days of steady riding, we made it to the river valley in the late afternoon. Looking down at the river, I felt a little apprehensive. Crossing a river was dangerous! Any number of things might happen—a horse could slip and lose its footing, step in a hole and fall, people could get swept away by a current or caught in an undertow—all of which could end in death for man or beast.

As we gazed at the flowing water, Moses spoke up. "I do not like the idea of crossing right now and going into the night wet, but I've got a bad feeling. I could have sworn I saw some dust behind us an hour or so ago. It was a few miles back, but I am not trusting enough of my fellow man to wait on this side of the river."

Looking at Celine, he asked, "Any tribes around this country hard to get along with? I know the Cree and the Assiniboine are friendly. Blackfoot should be a long way west yet, I'm a thinkin'."

Celine considered this for a minute. "The Gros Ventres used to travel through here, but that was a long time ago. They should be farther south but could be coming north to trade or hunt. They were allied with the Blackfoot for several years. Last we heard, that fell through. We heard talk of an alliance with them and the Crow."

"Then we'd better cross," Moses responded. "Being wet and cold is better than being warm, dry, and on foot. Or even dead."

We rode on an old trail to the riverbank. Weaving in and around brush and chokecherry trees, we made our way to the valley floor. The trail showed years of use by man and beast. For the last twenty yards or so, it zigzagged through some cottonwoods that seemed to grow quite well along the river. Once through the trees and onto the riverbank, we surveyed where we were to cross.

Moses said, "We got a problem here. The way that water looks, the horses will have to swim for a few yards in the middle. Which they can do, but our guns will get wet."

I thought out loud, saying, "There's lots of deadfall in them trees. Why don't we build a raft? We can tie one of our sleeping tarps over it. Then we put all the pistols and the Warner in my raincoat and tie it tight so it's as close to waterproof as we can make it. I will push it across and can swim behind it through the deeper water."

Moses and Celine both nodded in agreement. With Moses's tomahawk and some extra rope, we had that raft cobbled together in no time at all. Then we secured the tarp over it.

We wrapped the guns and bedrolls in our raincoats, tied the ends tight, and fastened the bundle to the raft.

The old mountain rifle and the smoothbore were too long to fit in the raincoat. Moses decapped both guns and then reached into his possible bag and brought out a steel bullet puller, a screw that threaded into the end of his ramrod. Dropping the ramrod down the barrel of the old rifle, he turned the rod and the screw bit into the soft lead ball. Once he felt it was in far enough, he pulled the ball out of the barrel. Lifting the long rifle up, he poured the powder into his hand and then put the powder back in his horn.

Taking the screw off his ramrod, he put it back in his possible bag. He next took out a steel worm. This looked like a spring that had been pulled apart and one end sharpened. It also threaded into the ramrod. This was used in the same manner as the screw, except it pulled a wadding from the smoothbore. Tipping the gun, the pistol balls and buckshot rolled out into his hand. He pulled another wadding and ended up with the powder in his horn, same as before.

Looking at us, Moses said, "I'll go first, then you swim the guns over. You'll have to return for the horses, and then you two can bring them over."

He started into the river. By now, the horses were used to crossing water, but we had never had to swim yet to get across. The two horses splashed into the river with little hesitation. When they hit the deeper water, Moses slid off and hung onto the saddle while the horses swam. It was only about twenty yards until the horses' feet made contact with the river bottom, and they could cross the rest of the way reasonably easy.

Now it was my turn. I started to unbutton my shirt, then uncertainly glanced over toward Celine. Sensing my embarrassment, she turned around while I quickly finished stripping down to swim across. I didn't need the extra weight and drag caused by clothes.

Then, I pushed the raft into the river. I gasped and sucked in my breath. My Lord, that water was cold! I started making my way across and kept pushing until there was no ground under my feet. The current caught the raft and started to move it downriver. For a sickening second, I worried that the raft was going to get away from me and we would lose all of our guns. I began kicking as hard and fast as I could, and I was slowly able to steer the raft around and push it toward the far shore. It seemed like a long time, but was probably only a few minutes until my feet could touch the bottom again. Moses ran to help me drag the loaded raft up onto the shore. I heaved a sigh of relief; we had gotten the guns across the river, safe and dry.

Moses started building a fire to dry everything out. While he made a rack to dry clothes on, I swam back across the river. Once on the other side, I put my clothes on. Then, riding one horse and leading another, I followed Celine across. There were a couple of shaky moments when the horse she was leading slipped and just about pulled her off her horse. Luckily, he quickly regained his footing, and when we hit the deeper water, he turned out to be a decent swimmer.

Once we were across, we went back a ways into the trees where Moses had a good-sized fire burning. Being as we were still on the floodplain, there was plenty of driftwood laying around as well as deadfall.

I quickly unsaddled the horses and hobbled them so they could graze. We unwrapped the pistols and bedrolls from the raincoats, and thankfully, they were all dry. We peeled off our wet clothes and hung them on the rack Moses had built, wrapping ourselves in our bedrolls to keep warm while our clothes dried over the fire.

Celine had taken our saddlebags off the saddles and brought them to the fire. All our jerky and hardtack had been wrapped in cloth and was damp. She set about drying it as best she could by making a rack out of green willows to set over the fire.

Moses and I set about looking after his rifle and the smoothbore. From his possible bag, Moses took out a small punch and screwdriver to disassemble both guns. Once everything was dry, we reassembled them. Taking some caps out of his bag, we fired three through each gun. This dried the hole in the nipple as well as any moisture left in the breech that our ramrods and cloth had missed.

By then, Celine had some of our meagre supply of food dried, and we started eating. At least with the dry air and the fire, our clothes had dried fairly quickly.

After a few minutes of silence, Moses started talking. "I spent a lot of years trapping in the Rockies. Counting the years I took your father with me, I figure about fifteen. Then we guided settlers to Oregon for seven years. I survived by trusting my instincts. And right now, I think we have someone following us."

Looking at Celine, he said, "You say the Assiniboine and the Cree have no quarrel with anyone around here? And the Ojibway aren't fighting anybody?"

Celine nodded. Moses continued, "Someone is on our backtrail, I'm sure of it. Can only be one of three things. Blackfoot are touchy, but we are too far east, so that rules them out. Gros Ventres should be farther south and west, but we can't rule them out. Or it could be more of Dixon's renegades."

I looked over at Celine. "Is this the only crossing in this general area?"

"There is one more, about ten miles south and a little west of here. It's not as good, but it is crossable."

Moses commented, "Six horses and our guns are certainly worth killin' for." Then, looking at Celine, he said, "Miss Celine, I hate to say this, but if they get you…" his voice trailed off.

Looking across the fire at Celine, I resolved no one was ever going to kidnap her again. I think she read my mind as she looked back at me. I did catch a faint trace of a smile.

Celine took first watch. We figured if anything were to happen, it would be later in the night or in the early morning, just before sunup. As it turned out, the night was uneventful.

Come morning, with our saddle blankets dry again after yesterday's crossing and our guns reloaded, we mounted up and headed out of the river valley onto the northern plains.

Now, some folks will tell you the prairies are flat. And farther south of us, they might be. But the country we were going through was slightly rolling, and there were lots of dips and draws that would hide an ambush. We had to be cautious. As a rule, I rode out in front fifty yards or so, Celine followed, and then fifty yards behind her, Moses covered the rear. There weren't many trees this far out from the river, and we were feeling really exposed.

Fortunately, it had been a wet enough spring that there were still some potholes with water in them. The first night after leaving the river, we were lucky enough to find water to camp beside.

It did not take long to set up camp, as we were travelling so lightly. After hobbling the horses and setting out our bed rolls, we sat around eating a little jerky and hardtack, of which we had about a week's worth left.

Moses figured we could use a deer or a buffalo calf first chance we got. An antelope would work, too.

We did not light a fire that night, lack of wood being one thing, plus we didn't need anyone seeing where we were camped.

Moses looked across at me and Celine. "Looks like the potholes still have a little water. We might get lucky and not have a long, dry stretch. How far till we get to the range of hills with good water and maybe some shelter?"

"Late, the day after tomorrow," Celine answered. "I do not like being out in the open either. Getting caught in a hailstorm, or even a heavy rain, would not be good."

Thinking aloud, I said, "Once today, when I was on a higher knoll, I thought I saw a puff of dust off to the southwest. I'm wondering, is there somewhere coming up, like a river crossing or a long deep ravine where we would have to ride south in order to keep heading west? And if so, is there a lesser-known crossing to the north that we could take? That way, we could avoid meeting up with anybody to the south of us."

Celine nodded. "We skirt the south side of a long chain of lakes. If the year is dry enough, there are some crossable places farther north in between some of them.

In a wet spring with lots of runoff, it can be one long lake going for miles to the north. It was not the wettest of springs this year, but far from dry. We either skirt the south side or run the chance of having to go north an extra half a day or more."

Moses commented, "I spotted dust southwest of us, too. Last thing we need right now is a fight. If one of us gets hurt or killed, we lose Judith. We cannot take the risk, even if it costs us a whole day. We've been lucky so far. And Judith is counting on us."

Celine and I agreed with Moses. We would angle a little more to the north and hope for a crossing spot in the middle of the lake, or lakes, as the case may be.

I found it hard to get to sleep that night, wondering what Judith was enduring. I just hoped she could hang on until we got to her. And how was Ollie managing? Had Pa's shoulder healed enough for him and Leonard to leave the fort yet?

Come sunup, we were already on our way. We had to be cautious until we had more information. Were we being followed? And if so, by whom? The only thing we could do was avoid a confrontation until it was on our terms. Hopefully, we were just being overly cautious, but who else would be out here travelling as quickly as us? No camp of Indians with wives and families or Metis with ox carts would be moving this fast, which left warriors looking for opportunities. Or renegades.

Chapter Sixteen

Sometimes you just get lucky. Angling a little more to the north, we had hit the trail before the sun was giving much light. It would have been impossible for anyone to see any dust we might have raised. Because of our concerns about being attacked, we ate a little pemmican while switching saddles and didn't stop to rest the horses. By early afternoon, our horses were at the point of wanting a drink and needing a rest. Looking ahead, we could see a break in the land. Riding up to have a look, we saw a long valley with water as far as we could see, which, due to the way the valley curved, was only a couple miles.

We rode down to the water, glad to find it was reasonably fresh. Celine had warned us that a lot of the water out here could be salty, especially if there had been a string of dry years.

After letting the horses rest and have a drink, we carried on, heading north along the lakes. About an hour before sundown, we found a narrows that split the lake. We crossed, let the horses have another drink, and kept going.

We rode for another couple of hours before making a dry camp in the dark, in a little hollow amongst some

The Long Ride

willows. The horses needed rest and time to catch up on their grazing. And we needed some shut-eye.

We started off sleeping with no guard. I had a big drink of water, so I would wake up about an hour past midnight. Some might say we were gambling, but with all Celine had been through, she needed a chance to rest. Moses was getting on in years, and I could see this trek was taking its toll on him as well, but he would never admit it. He would die before giving up.

I awoke and looked around. Hearing nothing, I made my way to the edge of the willows. Then, taking my time, I made a circuit, stopping for a few minutes to listen on each side. This was my routine until the stars said it was about two hours before sunup. Making my way back to the camp, I wasn't surprised to see Moses up, cradling his rifle. He was getting ready to go on watch.

"Anything going on?" he whispered.

"Nothing yet. We might be good tonight."

Neither of us figured we were out of the woods yet. But we had maybe gained some time on anyone trailing us. I went back to my bedroll and closed my eyes.

I awoke in the morning to see Celine standing close, looking down at me. She smiled warmly, saying, "Good morning, Jim," and then went to get her horse saddled.

Today, we would make the hill country where the springs were. Good water and green grass. The horses needed both, and we might find some meat walking around. Even this late in the season, Celine said that in the coulees, there would be some plants we could eat.

Rolling up my bedroll, I thought of Celine. Even after everything she'd been through, she could still smile. She never seemed to get rattled, no matter how tough things got. There was no denying that she had downright grown on me.

Once the horses were saddled, we checked the loads on all our pistols, mainly making sure the caps were all still tight on their nipples. Without a cap, most guns were just a club.

We set out with me in the lead, as we had been travelling for the past few days now. Looking ahead, I could see the land rising in the distance. The hills didn't just rise out of the prairie suddenly; the land just started to roll, and the rolls gradually got bigger until you could start calling them hills.

We entered the range of hills from the south, coming across a short chain of lakes with what appeared to be the highest part of the hills just north a mile or so.

We stopped at the first lake to water the horses. This lake looked fairly deep and clear. We had seen the odd slough on our way here, but the water in them didn't look very good; some appeared downright salty. This water was fresh. Celine told us her family had watered here in years past when hunting buffalo.

We followed the chain of lakes until we came out in an opening in the hills—sort of a pass, I reckon. There was a bigger lake ahead of us, but the shoreline was white with salt. Celine led us around the south end of the lake up to the opening of a long coulee that had a pretty good trickle of spring water flowing out of it.

This is where we would make camp and rest the horses for a day. As much as we needed to keep going, we were not going to get anywhere with rundown horses.

While Moses and Celine got down to the business of building a shelter, I put my saddle on a fresher horse and headed up the coulee. The bottom of the coulee rose slowly to the west end, where I had to ride up a steeper slope. As I came out over the top, I could see that I was surrounded by hills in all directions. It was hard to tell which was the tallest, the one to the northeast or the big one to the east. Man, this was country!

Looking south, I noticed another coulee; not as long as this one, but worth checking out. Tying my horse to a bush, I hiked over to see if there was a deer or maybe even an elk or antelope anywhere close.

Dropping down to my knees, I crawled over to the edge until I could look down in the coulee. There was a rise that created a fork at the west end. There was nothing in the fork closest to me, but toward the top of the south fork, I could see some deer at about 200 yards. This was a reasonably long shot, but I had hunted with the Warner enough to know that I could hit a deer at that distance. If I took the time to get any closer, the deer could get spooked and run off. The sun was already getting low; I was running out of daylight.

As I was watching the deer, a young buck stood up to stretch. Taking my time, I pulled the hammer back and took a careful sight. Aiming toward the top of his shoulder, I reckoned the bullet would drop enough at that range for a heart shot. I squeezed the trigger—BOOM. And when the smoke cleared, my deer was on the ground. He had gone about fifteen yards before he dropped. Riding over to where he lay, I took out my knife and commenced to dress him out, taking care to keep the liver.

Retrieving my horse, I hoisted the deer up and tied him on the saddle. And on foot, I led the horse back to our camp.

When I arrived, there was a nice little lean-to built and a fire going. Moses and I quickly skinned out the deer while Celine sliced the liver into thin strips and started cooking them on green willow sticks.

That liver was our first fresh food of any kind in days. While I had not been particularly fond of liver in the past, this was like eating one of my grandma's holiday suppers.

Once our meal was done, we quickly assembled a drying rack out of chokecherry trees and willow. By the light of the fire, we sliced up that deer and started the drying process. Hopefully, our fire wasn't visible for very far, as we were back in the coulee and had built our fire behind some brush and chokecherry trees.

Once our deer was all sliced up and put on drying racks, Moses went to his bed roll. Celine stayed by the fire, keeping an eye on the meat, and I picked up my carbine and hiked up to a good vantage point. The moon wasn't shining much, being obscured by cloud cover. Making my way to the top, I found a good place to keep watch by a large buffalo rubbing rock.

I kneeled on the ground, my eyes gradually becoming accustomed to the dark and my hearing getting used to the background noises. There were some frogs croaking down by the water, and a coyote decided to let the world know where I had dressed out the buck.

Everything seemed as it should. Being a calm night, I could hear our horses chomping on the lush grass of the coulee bottom. But then one of our horses stamped its foot, and the others started to act edgy as well. Horses just don't get uneasy for no reason.

Getting up off my knees, I wandered farther out from the rock and stood still, listening. It bothered me—it was as if I could almost hear something, but I couldn't pick out for sure what it was. But I knew it wasn't right.

Then it hit me. Off to the south, I noticed movement. I kept still as a small fox trotted right by me. Soon, there were more animals: antelope, deer, more foxes, and even the odd coyote scurried by.

Something was coming toward us! Still a long way out, but definitely heading our way. I hurried back to camp to warn the others.

Calling out to Moses and Celine as I got closer, I was surprised to find them already saddling the horses and putting our meat into saddlebags.

"We figured you'd be coming in fairly soon," Moses said as he finished readying my horse. "Had a deer go right by our camp. Celine has seen this before. I've heard about it but never saw it for myself. You are going to witness a buffalo herd on the move. But right now, we gotta get outta their way before they get moving good in the daylight."

After mounting up, we headed northwest, wanting to get as much distance as we could between us and the herd. I had no idea how far we would have to ride, as this was something new to me.

We rode until the sun started to cast its glow on the horizon. When we stopped on a hill to rest the horses and swap saddles, the sun was light enough to look back on the wide, flat valley we had just crossed.

There was a huge mass of brown moving over the hills from the south. A cloud of fine dust was travelling with them as they made their way onto the valley floor. We could hear the rumble and feel the vibration of thousands of hooves thudding over the ground. All along the horizon to the south and east of us were buffalo.

Celine warned, "We better keep moving. Our carts were caught in a herd one time, and it took two days to work our way to the edge."

As we made our way to the northwest, we came upon another range of hills. Celine called these the Neutral Hills. To the north was Cree territory, south and east Cree and Assiniboine. To the south and west were the Blackfoot, who may not always be in a friendly mood. Up to this point, most Hudson Bay posts had been built outside of Blackfoot territory. The tribe travelled to the forts to trade, not wanting the posts on their land. We were heading toward a trading fort called Rocky Mountain House, which was built just on the edge of Blackfoot territory.

When we stopped for our afternoon break, Celine dug some of the drier jerky from her saddlebags. I say drier, as we hadn't had the chance to finish drying it before we had to evacuate our camp. We would have to build racks and continue drying it tonight when we made camp, or it would start to rot.

I had been riding ahead most of the day. Toward late afternoon, Celine rode up to join me. It was nice having her ride there beside me. We didn't say much, each just enjoying the company of the other.

Once we made it to the edge of the hills, Celine led us to a good place to camp beside a pond. While Moses and Celine set up camp and commenced making a rack to finish drying our meat, I went on a scout around and found the highest point for miles around.

Looking back to the southeast, where we had ridden through a few hours ago, all I could see was grass and the hills. As my eyes got accustomed to the distance, I could see nothing to indicate anyone on our backtrail.

The sun was almost down, and the shadows were getting longer. I had pretty much decided there was nothing out there when a faint glint way off to the south caught my eye. It was the shortest and lightest of flashes, but still, it could mean bad news. This was getting spooky. Who could be following us? From all we had heard, we were reasonably sure that Dixon was north of us, heading for the gold fields at Barkerville.

The last of the meat was being put on the drying rack when I got back to the camp. Being in a hollow, I was fairly certain the light from our fire would not be visible for very far. Looking across the fire at Moses, I said, "I think our 'friends' are still behind us. I'm sure I just saw a flicker of light off to the south. I'm thinking they are in the hills just west of where we had our last rest stop."

Moses nodded, and for the first time, I realized how old my grandfather was looking. We had to get Judith back with this attempt, or I was going to be on my own, although I suspected Celine would not let me carry on by myself. But that worried me, too. I surely did not want her to be hurt or killed.

It was Celine who spoke up. "What if whoever is behind us..." She paused. "What if being behind us is just a bonus to them? You know, there were supposed to be more men joining up with Dixon than we've run into. What if he had someone in place to leave messages at one or more of the forts? A scout to lead them to a meeting place before entering the Yellowhead Pass wouldn't be hard to find, for a price. Having his plans change from taking land to taking over a 'gold rush' town would only encourage the type of men who would follow him."

Moses pondered for a minute, then spoke. "She just might be right. That would make getting Judith back a whole lot harder."

I thought about this. "How long would it take to get through these hills if we wanted to stay to the lower spots and have less chance of being seen?"

"We could head northwest. If we leave early, we would be into the hills far enough that we wouldn't be visible from the south by daylight." Celine continued, "Then we head west. With good weather, we would be crossing the Elk River in four days, possibly less. If we go north of Rocky Mountain House, we should hit an ancient trail, and a week to ten days later, we could be at the Yellowhead Pass. I remember my grandfather telling of this trail when he once made a trip with some Nor'westers to trade with the Kootenay. They left from Fort Edmonton but met some Indian traders where the trails met. I think he said they were Blackfoot from south of the Bow River."

"Say we gain time on our shadowers," Moses said, thinking aloud, "and get to the Yellowhead a day or even a half day ahead of them. With any luck at all, we should be in front of Judith and her kidnapper. We could then head east on the trail and ambush them. If the kidnappers are ahead of us, they would be waiting for the jaspers on our backtrail at the junction of the trails. We kill this Dixon and his scout, grab Judith, and head back toward Edmonton. Hopefully, without a leader, the rest won't follow us but rather head to the gold fields and, with any luck, freeze to death in the mountains."

Looking over to Celine, I asked, "Is there any reason that someone who has nothing to do with any of this could be on our back trail for so far? We've been covering ground as fast as humanly possible since we left Fort Qu'Appelle. No group of Indians is going to pass up a herd of buffalo this time of year. Bay traders are going to be on the trails. Red River carts couldn't keep up. Is there anyone that would have a good reason to be out here that could move this quick?"

Celine thought for a minute and then shook her head. "Not that I can think of."

Moses said, "Well, let's get some rest. That flash you seen was a ways off. If we're gonna be riding in about four hours, we all need to get some shut-eye. The meat will be dry by then. Our fire won't show down in this hollow. We can all sleep spread out back from the fire. The horses will let us know if something is wrong. We have to take the risk 'cuz tomorrow is gonna be a long day." When Moses finished talking, we all spread out our bedrolls and tried to get some rest.

Chapter Seventeen

Living on the trail as we had been for the last few weeks, we were used to getting up before sunrise. By the time the sun was up over the horizon, we already had the dry meat repacked in our saddle bags and a good five miles behind us.

By noon, we entered a gap that went through the highest of the hills and came out on the north side. Stopping by a slough of fresh water to give the horses a break and a chance for a little grazing, I told Moses and Celine that I would hike over to a rise in the land, figuring to see if there was anyone close to us.

Crawling the final few yards so as not to skyline myself, I managed to peer over the crest. It was clear—hills on my south side and nothing but rolling prairie for miles to the west and the north. I turned around to check our back trail; it looked clear as well. Looking again to the west and the north, I could see no movement. To my left, toward the hills, I could only see trees and grass. I started my way back to camp, stopping for one last look around. And then, I couldn't believe my eyes—there were fifteen to twenty Indians not more than 300 yards away from me, walking their horses out of a draw from the hills!

It took all the self-control I could muster to keep walking normal and easy back to Moses and Celine. I remembered Moses telling me never to show fear when dealing with Indians, as they respect bravery above all else.

They had been watching us for a while, no doubt about that. Now that they knew I was aware of them, what would they do?

Moses was waiting for me—standing, not moving, cradling his old Nazareth rifle in his arms. Celine was doing the same with the smoothbore. I went over and stood with them.

"She's your wife if anyone asks." Moses spoke just loud enough for both of us to hear, then muttered, "Oh hell, look at the quill work on their shirts. They're Blackfoot!"

The riders looked us over as they rode up. The ravages of smallpox had left pockmarks on many of their faces and arms. Still, these were proud warriors, well-mounted and carrying lances. I could see a few trade muskets, but a lot of them were armed with bows. This had to be a hunting party; we would already be dead if this was a war party. But things could still go south, and at this range, those bows would be fast and just as deadly as the muskets—not to mention a lance coming our way!

I had the flap undone on the army holster but made no move toward pulling my pistol. No need to get anybody excited. I remembered Moses saying years ago, there's a time for talkin' and a time for fightin'. I was pretty sure this was a time for talkin'.

A stocky middle-aged warrior approached us, stopping about ten yards away. His deerskin shirt had the most intricate quillwork on it, and judging by his air of authority, he seemed to be the leader. He started speaking to Moses in Blackfoot.

Moses answered back in a mix of Sign and Blackfoot. The leader looked at Celine and then said something to his men.

An older warrior, almost as old as Moses approached us. Looking at Moses, he said in slow English, "I know you, White Hair Killer of six Ree. I fought you in the Shining Times. I stole your horse and beaver furs."

Moses eyed the warrior. "I know you too, He Who Fights Big Bears. The way I remember it, I stole two of your ponies back."

The old Blackfoot laughed. "Those were good times. Should I take your horses today?"

Moses chuckled, "You can try. I have not fought Blackfoot for many years. Looks like there is almost enough of you to share the fightin' with my grandson."

The old Indian translated for the others. Some, I could see, laughed. So far, nobody was pulling out any guns; that was good. I knew I could get one of my pistols out in time to drop one or maybe two, Moses would get one with his rifle, and Celine might get a couple with the musket. That still left a whole lot of Blackfoot, and none of us, when the shooting was done. But none of them wanted to be one of the dead ones either. Maybe talkin' was gonna get us out of this mess.

Moses started speaking in Blackfoot, talking for what seemed like an eternity, and I noticed a change in the old warrior's attitude. He nodded a couple of times during the conversation. These were two old warriors speaking as equals. One was not superior to the other; maybe we had a chance.

Celine moved closer to me to reinforce the idea she was my wife. Whether it would make any difference to these fellers, I wasn't sure. We stood side by side, looking them in the eye. Any sign of weakness or that we might hesitate to shoot, and this would not go well for us.

After Moses and He Who Fights Big Bears had finished talking, the old warrior then went and had an animated conversation with the younger leader.

In a low voice, Moses told us, "They are a hunting party, and their camp needs meat. I told them where the buffalo are. The old man wants to go and get the buffalo. The leader wants to take our horses and the girl. He's being told six horses and a girl are not worth losing at least three or more warriors. I think the old warrior just might convince him. Keep looking them in the eye."

Moses continued, "I told him why we're here, and I think that might have helped sway him. But the younger one is the leader of this hunting party. He will have final say. This side of the hills is also Cree territory, so that could work in our favour. The Cree outnumber the Blackfoot these days. There is always a possibility some Cree could hear the shootin', and the Blackfoot don't want to start a fight with them either when they got hungry people to feed."

The warriors came back to us, and the young leader started speaking.

Moses translated, "We will go hunt the buffalo. Today is not a good day to fight. We have people to feed. We will water our horses and leave you."

He Who Fights Big Bears looked at Moses and laughed, "Another day, perhaps, I can steal your horses."

With that, the warriors dismounted and led their horses over to the water. We mounted up and headed west, not looking back. I rode close to Celine, keeping myself between her and the warriors. We exchanged a long look of relief. We knew how close we'd been to going under.

After we had been riding for a while, Moses started speaking. "We were lucky. Thirty-five years ago, we'd have lost our hair, and Celine would've had a new husband—if she was lucky. They didn't leave us alone 'cuz they were afraid. The three or four men they would have lost were needed a lot more than our horses. See, in the great smallpox epidemic of the 1830s, the Blackfoot lost close to two-thirds of their people. The Mandan and Hidatsa were almost wiped out. I heard from traders in the mountains that the Bay vaccinated thousands of Cree, Ojibway, and Metis. That's why the Cree are so strong now. They've pushed the Blackfeet back a hundred miles or more."

He continued, "Those warriors had people to feed, and looking after their people had to come first. Before the smallpox, they would've come out of those hills and hit us fast and hard. Probably killed you and me and took Celine and the horses."

Celine spoke up, "My grandfather was a trapper in the Shining Times, and he told me a story about the 'White-Haired Killer of Six Rees.' That was you? The story is true?"

Moses's eyes started to water slightly as his mind went back close to forty years. "Yes, it's true. Jim's grandmother is actually my second wife."

"In 1822, I saw an ad in a newspaper looking for a hundred men to go with Ashley's first fur brigade to trap in the Rocky Mountains. Now, back before then, there were trappers and traders in the mountains, mostly traders, mind you—Nor'westers and Bay men. Astor's American Fur Company was trading as well.

"We were to trap for the Rocky Mountain Fur Company. We were pretty green to the ways of the mountains, but those of us who survived learned fast. By the end of our second winter, we were pretty much part of the land.

"We would get resupplied at a rendezvous in the summer. That was the big event of the year. I remember one rendezvous was figured to have three thousand people: trappers, traders, Indians from various tribes, and some tenderfeet from the east."

Continuing, he said, "We would leave the gathering in time to be in a good trapping stream for fall. Five of us were wintering with the Shoshone, and that's how I met Pretty Wildflower."

Moses looked over and smiled at Celine. "There are many ways you remind me of her."

Then he took up the story again. "By the spring of '26, we were married. She stayed with me while I was trapping. We went to rendezvous that summer. Went trapping again in the fall and wintered with her family. Life was good."

Then his voice hardened. "Until the following spring. One morning, I had left before sunup and was setting traps in each stream I came across. I had ridden out around a mountain, following a good beaver stream. By the time I got back to our cabin, it was dark. All that was left was a pile of ashes, and Pretty Wildflower was dead. My spare horses and gear were gone. I cried for a day and then buried her."

Moses was silent for a few minutes. Celine and I remained quiet, not wanting to interrupt his thoughts.

He started to speak again. "The next morning, I saddled up and started following their tracks. Took me eight days to catch up with the killers, who turned out to be six Rees. Seeing as there was six of them, they felt safe, figuring one lone trapper wouldn't dare follow them, let alone attack them. I caught up to them near the headwaters of the North Platte. I was so set on revenge that I didn't even care if I survived.

"I watched them for an entire day, figuring out how I was going kill them. When darkness came, I slowly crawled up on the guard and took him out with my Green River. Killed two more with the knife before anyone even woke up. Threw the knife into another as he was getting up, shot one more with my pistol, and tomahawked the last one. I don't think it took thirty seconds. Unbeknownst to me, there was a trapper who came across the bodies a day later. By the next rendezvous, everyone in the mountains had heard about what had happened. I'd made no secret about my wife's murder and my revenge, and the other trapper had told all he had encountered. I became known as the 'White-Haired Killer of Six Ree.' People kinda left me alone for a while after that. For the next few years, the Rees tried to get me, but they gave up after losing a couple more warriors.

"I stayed in the mountains for a few more years, but it wasn't the same anymore. I finally left for Saint Louis, and that's where I met your grandma. She got me back on track. And you know the rest."

I looked over at Moses in wonder, saying, "Those Blackfoot even knew of you."

"They knew me. But don't ever think they were afraid; circumstances were just not in their favour. No Blackfoot warrior fears old white-haired ghosts from the past."

I never again mentioned anything about the killing of the Rees.

Chapter Eighteen

We rode for the rest of the day, only stopping once in the afternoon to rest the horses. By the time we had made camp in a low spot surrounded by silver willow, darkness was already falling. The Neutral Hills were still to the south of us, but we had been moving slightly to the north, so they were a few miles away.

We settled in for the night. Gazing up at the stars, I hoped Judith was seeing them too. Looking over at Celine, I caught her watching me. She blushed, then smiled. I grinned back at her.

"Wonder if them Blackfeet ran into whoever is on our backtrail?" I thought out loud.

"Been chewin' on that all afternoon," Moses answered. "It would make rescuing Judith a whole lot easier if them warriors would steal their horses and put whoever is follerin' us on foot. Sure be nice not to be worrying about our back trail. Celine, how many more days do you reckon 'til we're at the start of the Yellowhead?"

Celine wrinkled her brow, pondering for a few seconds. "If the going doesn't get too hard, I would think twelve days or so. Once we come to the forest, we will have to take a very old and little-travelled trail that follows the lay of the land. My grandfather travelled that way when he was young and looking for other passes through the Rockies for the Nor'westers. I am aiming for us to hit where he went, about thirty miles north of the Bay post at Rocky Mountain House. We could take an extra day and head to the post from here and pick up some supplies, but it is quite often abandoned in the summer. We could lose a day for no gain."

We all agreed that her original idea was the best. Leaving Moses and Celine to get some sleep, I walked out on the prairie to listen for anything that might be close. All I could hear was the occasional yip of a coyote. Once, a long way off in the distance, I caught the echo of a wolf's howl, but other than the odd rustle of leaves, it was quiet.

The unknown can be worrisome. Even something dangerous becomes something that can be dealt with, once it is known.

Making one last circuit around our campsite, I headed back to bed down. We were all reaching the point where we had to get some rest. Our horses were going to be needing a break. If we didn't find a good place to stop in the next two days—three at the most—we would be walking. We hadn't gotten much of a rest when the buffalo showed up the last time we had stopped. And our social gathering with the Blackfoot had drained us big time.

For the next two days, we rode, ate jerky, and slept. Midmorning on the third day, we descended into a narrow valley with a small river flowing east that Celine said was called the Battle River. We decided this was a good place to rest for a day and possibly pick some berries or wild vegetables.

We found a nice sheltered spot close to the river, and we set up camp. After we had the horses unsaddled and hobbled out to graze, we sat down and cogitated for a while. Moses looked at me and Celine, saying, "It's getting colder at night, and the farther west we go, the higher the elevation. It's already mid-September. We could start to have frost at night. And there's always a chance that the mountain passes west of the Yellowhead could be getting snow pretty soon. We need to get to Judith before they get caught in those mountains."

Taking stock of our meagre supplies, we figured we had about four days of jerky left. Celine reckoned we might still have eight or nine days of travel ahead of us yet, depending on how much we had to weave around swamps and hills. It was an ancient trade corridor we were heading for, which followed along the east side of the Rockies, and it was not going to be in a straight line.

As well as resting the horses, we needed to get more food. Celine found some reeds close to the river and started weaving some baskets. She had seen some chokecherry trees on our way down to the valley floor and wanted to pick some berries.

Moses and I split up, one going each way along the river, hoping to find something for meat. Deciding to climb higher so I could look farther up the river, I started to walk toward the rim of the valley. Staying off the skyline, I stopped and surveyed the landscape. As far as I could tell, we had this area of the valley to ourselves. Moving west, I came to a place where some taller silver willows grew over the crest of the hill. This would be the perfect spot to look over our backtrail.

Sheltering in the cover of the willows, I took my time looking around the whole area. I must have spent at least half an hour watching and waiting, but nothing seemed out of place. Maybe luck was on our side, and whoever was on our tail had run into a Blackfoot ambush.

I heard the boom of the old mountain rifle and knew that meant we would have meat. Working my way back to the east of our camp, I met Moses. He was carrying a dressed-out yearling buck that he said was a mule deer.

Celine had been busy while we were out, weaving two baskets that we could use for picking berries and carrying whatever greens she found.

Moses and I quickly built a drying rack and started cutting the deer into strips. Celine went off to pick some chokecherries.

I was cutting on a hind quarter when Moses asked, "See anything when you were up on top?"

"Not a thing, but that was almost an hour ago. I still think someone is behind us."

"So do I," he answered. "We can't risk a fight yet. I don't think they'll catch us any time soon; their horses will be just as tired as ours. Better go give the girl a hand with the berries. I can finish up here."

Grabbing my carbine, I headed over to the bushes where Celine was picking. She was on the far side of the berry patch, stripping clumps of the black fruit off the bushes. Looking at me, she smiled contentedly and kept on picking. With two of us working, we had the last basket filled in no time.

We walked back to the camp together. I have to admit, the more time we spent together, the more I liked her. But, with not having much experience around the female half of our species, I wasn't sure what to do about it. I think she liked me too, but I sure didn't want to do anything that would upset the apple cart. Maybe once we rescued Judith, I would have a talk with her.

We got back to find that Moses was done cutting up the deer. He had three fresh steaks cooking on sticks close to the fire, and the drying racks were full of strips of venison.

After we devoured our steaks, Celine insisted that we each eat a handful of chokecherries, telling us that they were full of nutrition and would help keep us from getting scurvy. We got them down, but man, they were bitter! Although there was a slight cherry taste to them.

Once the meal was finished, Moses and Celine turned in. I was on watch and kept the fire burning just enough to dry and smoke the meat. I would circle out and patrol around our camp, coming back to the fire every hour or so to add a few more cherry branches. Other than hearing coyotes howling and the odd owl hooting, everything was quiet.

Just before sunrise, Moses stirred and climbed out of his bedroll. "You get some sleep now. I'll take over watch."

As I crawled into my bedroll, I looked over at Celine, who was fast asleep. I realized I had two missions now: to rescue my sister, and to keep anything bad from happening to this girl.

I woke around midmorning to the smell of chokecherry smoke and drying meat. Looking around, I could see Celine had filled her baskets again with more chokecherries. As bitter as they were, scurvy would be a lot worse.

Moses made his way back to the fire as I was rolling up my bedroll.

"Thought you was gonna sleep all day," he laughed. Then, more seriously, he added, "I was up on top until a bit ago, and I didn't see anything. The horses have been resting since noon yesterday. This meat will be dry a little after high noon. I think we better get going once we have it packed up."

Looking to Celine as she walked back from washing in the river he asked, "This trail we're headed to, how far do you reckon it is till we hit it?"

"We should find it within two days. We keep going west until we reach the North Saskatchewan River. We'll want to cross it before any other rivers join it. Being this late in the year, we should be able to find somewhere we can get across. The farther south, the smaller the river is."

Moses questioned, "Are there other rivers after the North Saskatchewan?"

She nodded. "Yes. But the rest of the rivers flow east and northeast. So, the farther west you go, the easier they are to cross. After the North Saskatchewan, all of the rivers have good places to cross. The trail was used for centuries by people before they had horses."

She paused, then added, "Grand-pere told us that the trail stays out of the mountains and bigger foothills. This far north, it goes through a lot of forest. I just do not know how much. But I am sure that the trail is still the fastest way to the pass."

"They always are," replied Moses. "Those old Indian trails were made a long time before any white man seen these shores."

By the time the sun was at its peak, we were saddling horses. Once the jerky was packed, we hit the trail.

As far as we could tell, if there was anyone on our backtrail, they were still a ways behind us. They would find our campsite, but hopefully not for a few days. We were travelling too fast to hide our campsites or tracks.

We were starting to get into more trees but were still able to make good time, and in two days, we were looking across the North Saskatchewan River. Riding south, we managed to find a place that looked crossable by midafternoon.

Basically, it was a repeat of our earlier crossing of the South Saskatchewan, but with it being later in the year and closer to the mountains, this water was as cold as ice! I have never been as cold in my life as I was after we finished crossing that river.

Moses had a fire going by the time I came across with the last of the horses. With our clothes hanging on racks fabricated from aspen with Moses's tomahawk, we huddled close around the fire, wrapped in our bedrolls. It was a long time before we stopped shivering.

Once we were warm and dry, we went through the process of drying and cleaning our guns. That came first; our lives depended on those guns.

It was well past midnight before our clothes and saddle blankets were dried. We did not figure anyone would be crossing the river at night, so we all got a few hours of sleep. As I crawled into my bedroll, I realized that sometime in the last few days, it had been my eighteenth birthday.

We woke up to a frosty morning. We chewed some jerky, hardtack, and a handful of the chokecherries from Celine's stash then saddled up and headed out.

The trees were getting thicker now, but we could still ride in a northwesterly direction. It was later that afternoon that we came across a faint trail. How far back into the past this trail went, we had no way of knowing, but it had been used enough in the previous centuries that a scar was still visible.

Moses looked at the ancient travois marks. "This was used for a long time to leave marks like that. I'm sure I was farther south on this same trail forty years ago, way down in the Montana Territory."

"My Grand-pere told me it was in use long before any of the tribes had horses. He learned about it from an old Tsuut'ina—the Bay men call them the Sarcee." Celine continued, "It doesn't see as much use anymore, maybe because so many people have died in the epidemics and also because the Bay now has trading posts set up in so many places."

I took the lead and headed north up the trail. Celine followed, with Moses bringing up the rear. Now that we had found the trail, we just had to follow it until we reached the Yellowhead Pass.

For the next nine days we followed the same routine: rise early, get saddled, and hit the trail. We would eat some of our jerky while the horses rested, then swap horses, keep travelling, and make camp just before dark. Celine always managed to find a few greens to supplement our diet.

With all the trees and hills, we had no idea what was happening on our backtrail; we just had to keep moving.

It was going to be close, but I think we had gained enough time to intercept Dixon.

On the afternoon of the ninth day of following the ancient trail, we entered a valley running east and west through the hills. Celine looked around and pronounced, "This has to be it. This must be the start of the Yellowhead Pass. We're here!"

"We made it! All thanks to you, Celine." I beamed at her proudly.

"By God, girl, you got us here," laughed Old Moses. "Took us across five hundred miles or more of prairie and wilderness and brought us out right here. Your grand-pere would be proud!"

At this mention of her family, a shadow crossed Celine's face, and a tear slipped down her cheek. She then composed herself and said, "Now, let's go find Judith."

Wasting no time, we all spread out a couple hundred yards apart and looked for sign as we rode across the valley to the far side. We then joined back up and compared notes.

I started. "I didn't see anything even close to recent. Some unshod horse tracks, but they were days old."

Celine commented, "That's all I saw too. I think we are ahead of Judith."

"All I saw was them pony tracks," said Moses. "I think we should keep movin' and head east down the valley. We don't need that crowd behind us to catch up."

We all agreed that was the best course of action. The big question now was how much farther would we have to go before we met up with Dixon and Judith?

Chapter Nineteen

We made camp that evening by a small stream. Once the horses were taken care of, we sat around doing some figuring. There would be no fire tonight. Too much risk; aside from showing where we were, someone could smell it miles away if conditions were right.

We needed to come up with a plan. But not knowing how many men were with this Dixon, or even where we would cross paths, did not make it easy. Also burning in the back of my mind was the possibility that they had met up with and taken control of the people with the wagons that we'd heard about back in Fort Garry. We had a lot of variables to consider.

We all kinda figured that whatever we did would have to be done at night. Hopefully, there weren't too many men with Dixon. He had already abandoned one bunch, but as far as we knew, he had at least one scout with him.

"Celine," I asked, "Do you know anything more of this scout Mathias?"

"Mathias is one of those people who is just evil. He led the attack on my family." She was quiet for a minute, and I could see tears in her eyes. I reached out and put my hand on her shoulder.

Then, slowly, she started to speak. "There have been whispers among my people of murders that he has committed, but nothing has ever been proven. He can be charming if he wants something, but he is a vicious killer. However, as a plainsman or in the bush, he is one of the best. Probably as good as any of the Leveilles and they are some of the best scouts around."

"Here's how I figure it," Moses said after he finished chewing a piece of jerky. "If it's just a few on horseback, we hit them at night. I will take out the scout first. If he's on guard, that is good—two birds with one stone. If not, Jim, you kill the guard while I worry about the scout."

Looking at Celine, he continued, "You stay close to Jim. Let him take out the guard, then the two of you go get Judith. Jim might have to carry her, so you be ready to shoot anything that isn't me with that scattergun. Make sure you got your pistol. In the morning, we'll check all the caps on every gun."

"Now we need a plan in case they are with a group of wagons," I thought out loud. "Could be done in the daylight. We would need to be in a spot with some trees close enough that you could cover us. Celine and I would approach on our horses; we need Celine to point out Dixon. I'm thinking that he would probably keep Judith close."

Celine came up with an idea. "What if we were each leading a horse? That would get the attention of the bad guys more quickly than it would of people who are just going to the gold fields to prospect." She looked at Moses and me. "Unless there are no prospectors, and even the wagons are with Dixon."

"We will have to decide when we first catch sight of them. We might have to go in at night on the wagons, too. Could be some good people in those wagons, but if they aren't, that's a chance we'll have to take. We'll only get one shot at this, and we gotta make it good. We better get some shut-eye," concluded Moses.

Once Moses and Celine had bedded down, I took a walk out around our camp. Leaning against a tree in the dark, I listened intently but heard nothing out of the ordinary. After waiting a few more minutes, I went back to our camp.

Moses and Celine were both asleep. Finding my bedroll, I laid out where I could hear the horses. I lay awake, worrying about the upcoming confrontation and about what would happen to Judith if we failed. After all, we had no guarantees Dixon had even come this far. Or if Judith was even still alive. I eventually fell into a restless sleep.

Waking before sunup, I did a quick scout around the camp, moving quickly to get my blood flowing and warm up. By the time I returned, Moses and Celine were up and about. After chewing down some jerky and checking the caps on all our pistols, we saddled up and started riding.

We rode east all day, and still no sign. We spent another night shivering with no fire, then an early start the next morning. All three of us were feeling the tension; today could be the day.

Stopping for a break midafternoon, we had found a good spot to observe the trail from about a hundred yards. We concealed ourselves in a nice grove of aspens, their leaves already the yellow and orange of fall. The horses grazed in a little dip in the land behind us. We could watch the trail from here and still be close enough to take action, if need be.

As we finished chewing our dinner, Moses looked over to me and Celine. "Hopefully, we can get this done tonight. My old bones are telling me it's going to rain or snow sometime soon."

No sooner had he finished speaking than I detected movement off to the east. The shape of a wagon canvas came into view, followed by another, then another. Soon, five wagons were visible, heading toward us.

"Well, let's see what develops. We're in as good a place as any," Moses calmly observed.

Celine lay between Moses and me as we peered through the grass, watching the five wagons slowly approach. After what seemed like an eternity, the wagons finally rolled by us. We could tell something was not right. The drivers looked scared, their eyes nervously darting in all directions. And there were no women or kids. I had remembered MacTavish telling us that the prospectors had their families with them.

Then Celine gasped, "There he is, driving the middle wagon. That's Dixon!"

I looked over to where she pointed. I saw a tall man with dark hair and a beard, wearing a long grey coat with an officer's braid on the sleeves. There was no fear in this man; he held himself tall. There was no doubt who was in charge here.

I anxiously kept scanning the wagon train. "I haven't seen Judith yet. Have either of you?"

"Me neither. I'm betting she's in Dixon's wagon," Moses replied. Then, turning to Celine, he whispered, "Any sign of Mathias?"

She studied the group again, then shook her head. "No."

"That's a big problem. We need to know where he is," muttered Moses.

Rumbling past us, the wagons continued for another half mile before stopping and setting up camp. These people had been on the trail for quite a while. It was just a short time before the wagons were circled, and the horses were hobbled out to graze.

"We've got to see what's in that middle wagon," I speculated. "And where are all the women and kids?"

"Patience. Let's just watch. Maybe Mathias will turn up yet," cautioned Moses.

Celine turned her head to look at me, and her eyes opened wide! I spun around to see a man behind me, pistol in his hand. I reacted without thinking, drawing my knife and lunging toward him. He was lining up on me when I plowed into him, shoulder first. I swung my knife down, and it went in under his left arm. He still managed to fire his pistol, grazing me on my right side.

We both fell to the ground. I tried to slash at him with my knife again, but he pushed me away. He managed to rise to his knees. As he pointed his pistol at me again, I thought I was a goner. Then he suddenly collapsed to the ground, gurgling, with Moses's old Green River buried deep in his throat.

I laid on my back, gasping for air. That was close! My legs were weak as I tried to stand.

Celine opened my shirt to see where I'd been hit. The bullet had just nicked the skin, nothing serious. A bandage would do for now.

Moses looked down at the dead man. "I sure hope that's Mathias."

"It is," Celine answered in a low voice. "It's Mathias."

Still gasping for breath, I managed to say, "What about that shot? They would've heard it."

Moses pondered out loud. "One pistol shot. Just one shot. If I was Dixon, I'd be thinking 'Mathias must have found something. But what?' Dixon knows he has to stay by the wagons to keep the others under control. And it'll be full dark in less than an hour."

I looked down at Mathias's carcass. "He is about the same size as me. His shirt is all blood, but my shirt should be close enough to pass. If I put on his pants and hat and we find his horse, I could ride toward their camp and maybe get close before I was found out."

"And then get shot?" Celine snapped. "That is a bad plan."

"What if you were on his horse and following me at gunpoint, like I was your prisoner?" Moses interjected. "We'd have our pistols, I got the Remington, and we still got that extra Colt. I could put both in my belt."

"That could get you both shot! At least take me with you. I could have the musket hanging on my back. They killed my family!"

"I don't want you shot." I was trying to argue a losing battle.

"They won't shoot me intentionally. I'm valuable to them. I'll have a pistol and the musket. I'm going with you, Jim Munro."

Moses looked at me. "Think ya lost that one, Jim. Let's go before it's too dark."

Not wasting any time, Celine went looking for Mathias' horse while I got changed into the dead man's buckskin pants and put on his battered hat. She returned in a few minutes, leading the horse.

Moses looked me over. "You'll pass. They won't see us clearly 'til we're close."

"What if I'm challenged before we are close enough?"

"Speak slowly, with a strong French accent, and you might just get away with it," Celine answered.

"Okay, let's go." I felt like Daniel going into the lion's den as I mounted that horse.

We moved out of the trees and started toward the wagons. The light was fading fast. I could make out people, but not colour. Six hundred yards to go. No challenge yet.

My 'prisoners' kept walking ahead as I followed on Mathias' horse, covering them with my carbine. There was a trade rifle in his saddle scabbard, which I had left in place.

Halfway to the wagons, I could now see people moving around, but still, no one challenged me. Moses and Celine kept walking, ever closer. No man had ever gone into battle with braver companions; I was certain of that. We just needed to come out of this alive.

Two hundred yards; we kept going. Another fifty. There must be guns pointed at us now. We kept moving, ever closer. The light continued to fade. We headed toward the wagon that hopefully, Judith was in.

At fifty yards someone hollered, "Mathias, that you? Who do you got there?"

Celine whispered, "That's Dixon."

"Oui, c'est moi." My best attempt at a French accent got us to within fifteen yards.

I saw a pistol flash up in his hand. God, he was fast with a pistol! A burst of red flame came toward me. I felt like I'd been hit with a sledgehammer, low on my left side, as I swung my Warner in his direction and fired. Through the black powder smoke, I saw him spin around, but he kept moving.

A tall, gaunt-looking man, wearing the tattered remains of a Rebel uniform, came around the nearest wagon. He had a rifle in his hands pointed right at us. Before he could even squeeze the trigger, there was a loud BOOM, and a long blast of orange flame came from Celine. She had got the musket out from under her jacket and blew that attacker to hell.

Moses had moved over to the left. He was firing his pistol toward the muzzle blasts that were coming from behind the next wagon. The air hung heavy with smoke and the acrid smell of burnt gunpowder.

I could still see muzzle flashes coming at me and hear bullets winging by my head. I had my pistol in my hand by now. Remembering Pa, I took that extra fraction of a second to be sure and put another bullet into Dixon. He hit the ground this time.

I was off my horse now, running to the right and skirting around another wagon. Despite the smoke, I could see that there were two gunmen shooting at Moses and Celine. I let off a shot at one and heard him scream as he took a ball in the ribs. That got the attention of his buddy, who spun around with his raised pistol, firing at me. The bullet hit hard above my right knee, and I staggered. Managing to stay on my feet, I pulled out my other pistol—the Whitney—and fired three times in quick succession at the second gunman before collapsing to the ground.

It was quiet.

Then Celine was kneeling beside me, tears in her eyes. "Don't you die, Jim Munro. Don't you dare die on me!"

Looking into her worried eyes, I pulled her head down and kissed her. "Girl, I have wanted to do that for weeks. There's more where that came from, but for now, help me up so we go can get Judith." Celine helped me stand up, and I leaned on her as we made our way over to Dixon's wagon.

Moses was already opening the wagon canvas by the time we got there. He leapt inside and hollered, "She's here! She's alive!"

A rush of relief burst over me. Judith was alive! We'd done it! We'd found her. I had never felt so happy in my life.

Moses climbed down out of the wagon, carrying Judith in his arms. She was sobbing and clinging to him. She was thinner, and her dress was stained and torn. She had dark circles under her eyes, and I could see bruises on her face. But even now, she had tried to keep herself tidy and had her hair neatly tied back with a leather strap.

I then noticed the rope burns on her wrists, and my blood started to boil.

Judith lifted her head off of Moses's shoulder and looked around. Her eyes fell on Celine, and she exclaimed, "You're okay! How did you get away?" Then she spotted me. She gave a cry of delight, followed by a horrified, "Jimmy, you're bleeding!"

"I'll be fine; don't you worry. Celine will patch me up. She's getting used to treating bullet wounds on us Munros."

Judith looked around behind me. Seeing no one else, her face turned white, and in a trembling voice, she asked, "Where's Pa?"

"William is just fine," Moses said. "He caught a bullet when we rescued Celine, but she took care of him. We left your Pa at Fort Qu'Appelle, but I imagine we'll be running into him before we get to Fort Edmonton."

"Did you bury Ollie?" Judith quietly asked, with tears in her eyes.

Moses grinned as he gave her the good news. "Well, he didn't want buried last we seen him. He was on a Red River cart being hauled home for your grandma to doctor back to health. He was alive when we left. He had crawled for a long way with a bullet in him, follerin' after you. Your Pa came across him after he had collapsed."

Judith cried out joyfully, "Thank God he's alive!"

Then her face turned dark. "Where's Dixon?" she demanded.

One of the wagon men had come over to us by now. He pointed to where Dixon was lying on the ground, moaning. "He's over there. And still breathing."

Looking at me, Judith grimly asked. "That pistol got any bullets left in it?"

"I think it's still got three."

Her face darkened, and her jaw set. She took the gun from my hand and very slowly and deliberately made her way over to where Dixon lay bleeding. He'd taken my carbine bullet on his lower right side and had caught my pistol ball below the left knee. He struggled to rise, but his leg wouldn't hold him, and he collapsed back to the ground.

He glared at her through his distinctive eyes, angrily sneering, "I should have just let my men have their way with you."

Judith coldly looked down at the man who had disrupted her life and caused so much misery. "You need to know—my husband is alive." Pointing the Whitney at his right knee, she took careful aim and fired. "That's for Ollie."

Dixon shrieked with pain. He yelled, "I would have treated you like a queen!"

Gazing down at him with disgust, Judith pulled the hammer back on the pistol and took aim. She fired again, this time shattering his left shoulder. "That's for Celine's family."

And then, pointing at the middle of his chest, she deliberately fired the last round. "And that's for me."

Not even glancing at his crumpled carcass, she turned her back to him and walked toward us then sank down to the ground in complete mental and physical exhaustion.

Looking down at Judith, I couldn't have been more proud of her. Her spirit and determination had brought her through this ordeal. But it sickened me to see the toll it had taken on her.

Moses gently scooped up Judith and carried her over to a wagon. The wagon driver helped him lay her down on some blankets and covered her up warmly. She fell into a deep sleep.

I suddenly felt lightheaded and nearly fell over. Celine looked at me and exclaimed, "We've got to take care of those wounds." She led me over to another wagon and went to work plugging my bullet holes.

In the meantime, Moses was over talking with the wagon men. Dixon had got the jump on them early one morning and took over. He had disarmed the men by holding their wives and kids hostage. Then, four days out of Fort Edmonton, he had abandoned the wives and kids to fend for themselves on the trail.

The men wanted to hitch up and head back to their families right away. But Moses managed to convince them to wait till morning so the horses would be rested. He warned them that we might not be out of the woods yet, as more renegades could still be coming down the trail. He had them gather up all the guns from Dixon's men, and they commenced cleaning and reloading everything.

I missed out on all of this, as I had passed out when Celine was digging out the bullet I had acquired in my side.

I awoke the next morning in a moving wagon. The first thing my eyes focused on was the prettiest sight I had ever seen—Celine.

She smiled down at me. "You're going to be okay."

"I should hope so. I doubt you'd marry me if I was dead," I teased.

She bent down and gave me a big ol' kiss. "I'll marry you, Jim Munro."

Chapter Twenty

Moses had laid out the carcasses of Dixon and his men so that anyone coming down the trail would see them. Then, he organized the wagon drivers and handed out the guns, making sure everyone was armed.

We'd stopped for the night and set up camp after our first day on the trail. After supper, Moses, Celine, Judith, and I were gathered around the embers of the fire.

Judith started to speak slowly. "They hit our place early in the morning. I was cleaning up in the kitchen after breakfast, and Ollie was out in the barn, tending to the horses. I heard a gunshot from out in the barn and then heard men running toward the house. I grabbed Ollie's rifle and was pointing it toward the door when they came busting through. I shot one of them, but the rest grabbed me and were trying to pin me down on the table. Then Dixon came in. He pushed the others off of me, saying, 'She's for me.'

"He ordered them to tie me up. I cried out for Ollie as loud as I could, and then one of them backhanded me so hard I passed out. When I came to, I was tied up in the back of the wagon, and we were moving. I had no idea who these men were or where we were going.

"When we stopped for the night, Dixon untied my hands and brought me some food to eat. I begged him to tell me what had happened to Ollie. He told me that Ollie was dead, but as long as I behaved, nothing would happen to me. He re-tied my hands and left. I cried myself to sleep that night."

Judith paused, and I stood up to throw another chunk of wood on the fire. When I sat back down, she started speaking again.

"They kept me in the wagon for days. Dixon would come and let me out a couple times a day so that I could relieve myself. Most nights, if we were camped by water, he would let me wash. That's when I got the idea of leaving messages for you."

She turned to Moses. "Did you see any of my signs?"

Moses said, "We did, Judith. And that was mighty good thinkin'. That's how we knew we were on the right trail."

Judith nodded. "That's all that kept me going, knowing that you would be coming after me."

Judith took up her story. "The days all seemed to blend together. Until one morning when I heard gunfire and screams." And then, looking over at Celine, she said, "That's when you were thrown into the wagon with me.

"We could hear them arguing outside. The men wanted to take us to Fort Benton and sell us to a brothel. When Celine and I heard that, we almost gave up hope."

Celine nodded as she and Judith exchanged a long glance.

Judith went on, "We could tell that Dixon was losing control of this crowd. So it didn't surprise me when he grabbed me out of the wagon in the middle of the night. We headed out on horseback. He said we were going to the gold fields at Barkerville and that the scout Mathias knew the way. And that when we got to Barkerville… he was going to marry me."

I stared at her in disbelief. "What?!"

Judith paused a moment, gathering her thoughts. "In his twisted mind, Dixon considered himself a southern gentleman, above taking a woman forcefully. He honestly couldn't see why I wouldn't jump at the chance of marrying him. I had seen what happened to the men who disagreed with him. So I just quietly went along with him, never actually committing to anything, and prayed that you would find me in time."

She looked over at us again and said fervently, "And thank God you did."

"Outside of Fort Edmonton, Dixon managed to pick up a few more men, bribing them with talk of gold. A few days past Fort Edmonton, we came across this wagon train of prospectors and their families who were heading to Barkerville. Dixon and his men commandeered the wagons and the drivers, abandoning the women and children."

Judith took a deep breath and continued. "The closer we were getting to Barkerville, the more Dixon was pressuring me to accept his proposal. I finally snapped, 'It'll be a cold day in hell before I would ever marry you!'

"His face turned red, and he flew into a rage, slapping me across the face. He threatened, 'You'll either marry me, or I'll sell you to a brothel.' He then threw me into a wagon, tying up my hands again.

"I knew that I had kicked a hornet's nest by finally speaking up to him. And all I could do was hope that you found me soon."

Moses finally asked the question that had worried him ever since Judith had been abducted, "So he didn't mess with you? Dixon, or any of his men?"

Judith shook her head and said, "No, they didn't. But I don't know how much longer I could have held Dixon off after he blew up at me." We all sat quietly for a few minutes, her words hanging in the air. We were thankful that she had been spared that, at least.

There was nothing more to say after that. Moses stood up, saying, "I'm going to go check with the guys on watch, make sure everybody's on their toes. You all go get some sleep."

Chapter Twenty-One

Judith seemed to be recovering as well as could be expected from her ordeal and had taken to riding one of the extra horses we'd acquired. Celine would ride with her when she wasn't busy fussing over me.

It was on day four, at the noon time rest stop, that our shadows finally showed themselves. Moses had been behind us, checking our back trail, when he came galloping into our camp. He stuck his head in the wagon as Celine was changing my bandages. "Are you able to shoot? Our friends from our backtrail have showed up."

"I can shoot, all right. You just tie back that canvas and hand me my carbine."

"Figured you would. Some of these prospectors are vets, so we got a chance. I counted a dozen renegades. They look in mighty rough shape." With that, Moses went to prepare everyone else.

Judith climbed up and joined me and Celine in the wagon, and we all settled down to wait.

They appeared from the west, walking their horses toward us. They stopped at around 300 yards. One of them rode up closer, wearing the faded, dirty remains of a Union uniform with what appeared to be a white rag tied on a Springfield rifle.

Stopping at halfway, he hollered, "Customary to meet halfway."

"You're halfway. So speak your piece," yelled Moses.

"We just need some food and a couple of horses, and we'll leave you alone. Dixon's dead, so I guess his grand ideas went with him."

"His grand ideas died the day he kidnapped my granddaughter. And most of his men died too. You fellers is all that's left of his 'army.' You want to join the others, we'd be happy to oblige ya. We need our grub for us. Even if we did leave you a few days' worth, you fellers would just find someone else to rob and kill. So go to hell."

The renegade turned and rode back to the other riders. Then they just sat on their horses and watched us.

Moses had the wagons moving again, travelling side by side, spaced with a few yards between them.

The tattered remains of Dixon's army followed about 500 yards behind. Looked to me they were a little unsure of what to do next.

Then, the reality set in on these men. We were not going to let them come and take anything. They were hungry, on worn-out horses, and desperate, long past any concept of making an honest living. They had been promised riches, and nothing had panned out. They did the only thing they knew. The riders spread out in a line, then started toward us at the trot. At 300 yards, they broke into a full gallop.

By now, Moses had already stopped the wagons. Off to my left, I heard the roar of his old Nazareth, and one of the riders dropped out of his saddle. I had my carbine centred on another renegade. He, too, fell off his horse after I fired.

The prospectors let them come closer and closer and then opened fire. Two more saddles were empty. I reloaded and fired again. A rider slumped in his saddle but stayed mounted. It looked like some were still going to make it to our wagons.

Suddenly, there was a shrill whistle, followed by a boom from way out to our left. Another rider crumpled to the ground. Pa and his deputy, Leonard, had caught up to us! And it couldn't have been at a better time!

In the meantime, Moses had reloaded and fired at another renegade. He fell. The last five of Dixon's army had had enough and broke off the engagement, wheeling their horses around and heading back west.

There was another shrill whistle and a loud boom, and a hat flew off the head of one of the fleeing riders. Apparently, he wasn't too worried about it because he didn't even look back; he just kept on a'riding.

After the riders were well out of shooting range, I looked to our left as Pa and Leonard rode up to meet us. God, was I ever glad to see Pa again!

Judith bounded over to get a big hug from Pa. For the first time in my life, I saw tears in Pa's eyes, and they were tears of pure joy. It was a long time before they let go of each other.

In the meantime, Celine was helping me climb down from the wagon. Pa looked over to us. "Mighty good to see you, son. Looks like you're a little worse for wear, but as I can vouch, I know you've got a good little nurse there."

Grinning and looking back at Pa, with my arm still around Celine, I said, "Yes, sir. And we got Judith back."

Moses rode over to us and, beaming at Pa, said, "Well, look who showed up, and just in the nick of time? Ain't you a sight for sore eyes?"

Pa replied, "Glad to be here."

Now, the prospectors were hurrying over to Pa. "Have you seen anything of our families?" they anxiously asked.

"They're just a couple of days down the trail," Pa replied. "They were cold and hungry when we met up with them. We built a big fire and loaned them our blankets. We left them all of our provisions and our pack horse. They won't be living high on the hog, but they will be alive."

With that, we headed out toward Fort Edmonton with Pa and Judith at our sides.

EPILOGUE

The trip back to Fort Edmonton seemed like a downright pleasant journey after what we had all been through these past weeks. We were just two days down the trail when we witnessed the happy reunion between the wagon men and their families.

We had a lot of catching up to do with Pa and Judith. Of course, I had Celine looking after me like a mother hen. I think Pa was starting to wonder if she would ever let me get around on my own.

Moses didn't let Judith out of his sight. No one was ever gonna take her again.

We reached Fort Edmonton and stayed there for a few days to rest and recover before we hit the trail again. With the help of some of Celine's cousins, we made it back to Fort Garry by the last week of October.

After giving him a full report, Governor MacTavish insisted that we all stay with him for the night, treating us to a royal feast. The next morning, we handed in our commissions. Then, bidding him farewell, we mounted up and headed for home.

I will never, as long as I live, forget that homecoming. Ollie and Grandma were standing on the porch as we rode up to the house, snow lightly falling on us. Ollie raced over to Judith and swung her off her horse. Then he swept her up in a big hug, both crying tears of joy.

Grandma greeted the rest of us as we stepped onto the porch, giving each of us a hug, including Celine. As she hugged Moses, she whispered, "I knew you would bring our girl home." Then she briskly exclaimed, "Let's get inside, out of this cold!"

I stayed on the porch for a moment, looking around the yard and contemplating all that had happened. It had been three months since we had ridden out of here, but it felt like a lifetime ago. We had faced renegade bullets, bears, buffalo, and Blackfoot warriors, doing whatever we had to to get Judith back. I had left a boy and come home a man.

Turning around, I then went inside to the warm fire—and Celine.

Our long ride was over.

GLOSSARY

Aquavit – A distilled spirit produced in Scandinavia, which is often drunk during festive gatherings.

Breech-loading – A gun that is loaded at the rear of the gun barrel.

Buckshot – Small round pellets made of lead.

Calibre – The measurement of the width of a bullet, or a round lead ball, in 1/100s of an inch.

Carbine – A firearm with a shorter barrel—usually around 20" long—which was issued to the cavalry.

Cartridges, metallic – A metal case made of brass or copper, which contained the primer, the gunpowder, and the bullet. Used in the breech-loading guns which came out during the Civil War.

Cartridges, paper – Used in the infantry rifled muskets. The gunpowder and minié bullet came wrapped together in greased paper. The soldier bit the end off the paper, poured the powder down the gun barrel, then pushed down the bullet with his ramrod.

Casting bullets – To make bullets by heating lead in a small pot and pouring it into a mould.

Coulee – A deep ravine.

Cylinder – The cylinder is the cylindrical, rotating part of a revolver containing multiple chambers. In the case of this book, each chamber held powder and a greased ball.

Flintlock – A firearm that uses a flint-striking steel to create a spark to ignite a small amount of black gunpowder in a pan on the outside of the gun. This causes a small flame to enter a little hole into the barrel, which ignites the main charge. Flint guns date back as far as the 1500s and were the main ignition system up to the 1820s.

Greased patch – A piece of cloth, often soaked in animal fat, that was wrapped around a lead ball so that it fit snugly in the rifling of the gun. This caused the ball to spin when the gun was fired, increasing its accuracy as well as creating the necessary gas seal for the gunpowder.

Green River Knife – A favourite of the mountain men, these knives were made in Greenfield, Massachusetts, by J. Russell.

"He-coon" – An early American term for a wily old man who you would never want to mess with.

Hobble – To tie the front legs of a horse together close enough to prevent it from straying away.

Kepi – A wool peaked cap worn by both armies in the Civil War; Union being blue, Confederate being grey.

McClellan saddle – A cavalry saddle adopted in 1859 and used for the remainder of the horse cavalry days.

Minié bullet (also called minié balls by soldiers) – A hollow base bullet, slightly smaller than the rifling in the gun, so that it would slide down the barrel easily, even if the barrel was fouled with powder. When fired, the force of the powder would expand the hollow base into the rifling, so the bullet would come out spinning for greater accuracy.

Muzzle – the front end of the gun barrel.

Navy Colt – A .36-calibre handgun manufactured by Colt.

Nazareth mountain rifle – These were large .54-calibre rifles with full-length stocks produced by various gunsmiths around Nazareth, Pennsylvania. They were used by the mountain men who went west to trap beavers circa 1820. These rifles could weigh up to fourteen pounds.

Nipple – The nipple is a cone with a hollow conduit through it that directs the explosion from the percussion cap to the gunpowder.

Percussion cap (commonly referred to as cap) – A small copper or brass cylinder with one closed end. Inside the closed end is a small amount of a shock-sensitive explosive.

Picketing – Tying horses to a tree or stake with a long rope so they can graze freely.

Pilgrim – Slang for inexperienced newcomers.

Pistol – Handgun.

Possible bag – A leather pouch used to carry tools and accoutrements necessary for the maintenance and firing of a mountain rifle.

Powder charge – The amount of gunpowder used to fire the gun.

Primer – In Civil War metallic cartridges, the primer was the explosive in the rim of the cartridge. When it was hit by the firing pin, the primer would explode, causing the gunpowder to ignite.

Ramrod – A long round rod used to push balls down the barrel of a rifle or for cleaning the rifle barrel.

Reb sniper rifle – See Whitworth sniper rifle.

Ree – How mountain men referred to the Arikara Indian tribe.

Rendezvous – An annual summer gathering in the Rocky Mountains, where the fur trappers and Indian tribes could trade and exchange goods with the trading companies.

Revolver – A handgun that commonly has one barrel and uses a revolving cylinder containing multiple chambers for firing. Often also referred to as a six-shooter.

Rifle musket – The most common weapon of the infantry soldier in the American Civil War. It had a 37 – 40" long rifled barrel with an average weight of nine pounds. They included Springfields, made in the USA; Enfields imported from England; and the Lorentz, imported from Austria.

Rifling – Spiral grooves cut inside the barrel of a gun to make the bullet spin, thereby improving accuracy.

"Seeing the elephant" – Civil War soldiers referred to being in combat as having "seen the elephant."

Shining Times – An Indian reference to the era of the mountain men, from before 1820 to the mid-1830s, when they were trapping and trading with the fur companies, and life was good.

Smoothbore musket – Older guns that were still in use during the Civil War, with smooth barrels that had no rifling.

Stock – The wooden part of a gun to which the barrel and firing mechanism are attached. On older military weapons, the stock went the full length of the barrel.

Travois – A type of sled used by North American Indians to carry goods, consisting of two joined poles pulled by a horse or large dogs.

Warner carbine – One of the many single-shot breech-loading carbines that came out during the Civil War.

Whitney Navy revolver – a .36-calibre handgun manufactured by Eli Whitney Jr.

Whitworth sniper rifle/ Reb sniper rifle – A rifle made in England patented by the Whitworth Company in 1854 and issued to Confederate snipers. The interior of the barrel was hexagonal with a twist and used a corresponding hexagonal bullet, thus causing their bullets to make a distinctive whistling sound.

Yankee double eagle – A $20 American gold coin.

www.ingramcontent.com/pod-product-compliance
Lightning Source LLC
LaVergne TN
LVHW040144080526
838202LV00042B/3022